ETERNAL NIGHTFALL

BY BAYLI PECK

This is a work of fiction. Names, characters, places, and incidents either are the product of the author's imagination or are used fictitiously. Any resemblance to actual persons, living or dead, events, or locales is entirely coincidental.

Copyright © 2024 by Bayli Peck

All rights reserved. No part of this book may be reproduced or used in any manner without permission of the copyright owner except for the use of quotations in a book review.

This hardcover edition first published in 2024

Book design by Bayli A. Peck

ISBN 979-8-3385-3968-2 (paperback)

ISBN 979-8-3385-3343-7 (hardcover)

Published by Bayli A. Peck

Eternal Nightfall

BAYLI PECK

For Layla,
Thank you for motivating me and pushing me to write this book.

Chapter One

I winced in pain as Damian landed a blow to my stomach. I bent over, and once I did, he delivered a punch to my face. I struggled, got back up, and grabbed the cross I had buried deep inside my pocket.

"FATHER," I began, "PUT A BUBBLE OF PROTECTION TO WARD OFF THESE EVIL SPIRITS AROUND ME, AMEN."

As I said this, a bright light circled me.

"AAH-" Yelled Damian

With my limited time, I kicked a blow to his knees. As he fell, I pushed him.

I could see the fear in his eyes as he stumbled back to the ledge. As he attempted to regain his balance, he recited a spell of black magic. As soon as he finished, he fell off the edge of the Core. I winced in pain at the spell but soon felt a warm aura around me; it was finally-

So, you're probably wondering who I am and how I got here. Well, my name is Flynn, and I'm 14. It was a typical week: getting groceries, going to work, trying to survive in an economy that was casually collapsing, and trying to get around the education crisis. You know, standard stuff. But then, that's when it all began. To my surprise, it was only the beginning.

The beginning of the end.

"Hey, Mr. Evans!" I greeted Mr. Evans as I crossed the pavement, returning the groceries to my house.

"Hey Flynn! Say, how's Ness?"

"Oh, he's just fine, sir! Why he's just starting the 4th grade, a smart one he is. Maybe he'll make it to the 10th."

"Let's hope so!" Mr. Evans laughed, "Well, have a good day, son!"

"Thank you, sir, you too!"

I hummed as I made my way back to my house. It's a good day— I thought to myself—you can almost see the sun!— I fumbled with the groceries I was holding, trying to grab the keys to my house. Right before I could grab my keys, I heard the lock turn from the inside of my house. "Flynn! You're home early!" Exclaimed my younger brother, Ness. "Hey buddy, you are too!" I stepped inside my house and put the groceries on the counter. "Yeah," Ness began, "they had to cut school early today; one of the students who ventured too far from the barrier still wasn't found. It's been two months now! Poor girl, I knew her too, and actually, I think you knew her, too. Her name is Millie?" I awkwardly laughed as I was putting the groceries away. I did know her; we were in the 4th grade together. She was a nice girl, but we stopped talking after I dropped out to start working. "Whatever you say, dude. Can you help me put some stuff away? I got off work early so I could go shopping a little." Ness nodded quickly and began helping me put groceries away. You could feel the tension in the air; it must be because of the date.

You see, five years ago today, life became a literal Hell. I still remember it like it had just happened…

4/15/50XX...

"Flynn...." Mom began, "What did I say about eating cookies, young man?" I giggled and ran off to the dinner table, hearing Mom mutter while laughing under her breath.

"Hey Flynn?"

"Yes, Momma?"

"Please grab Ness and bring him to the dinner table."

"Okay!"

I jumped off the chair and walked towards where Ness was playing with his toys.

"C'mon' Ness, it's dinner time." I grabbed Ness by his hand and led him back into the kitchen. I picked him up and put him in the chair next to mine.

"Okay, kids," Mom began, "let's say grace."

We all bowed our heads down in unison, and my mother began the prayer. I opened my eyes and tilted my head upwards to see my family saying grace. I saw my brother, who was simply playing with his toys. I smiled at the sight of it. Then I saw my mother. Her expression was intense and bold, as if her life depended on prayer. Startled, I put my head back down and shut my eyes tightly. After we finished the prayer, we began to eat.

That's when we heard the rumble.

At first, we thought it was merely an Earthquake, for we had lived in California, so it was typical for us, but soon, we realized it was much more than that. The rumbling started to get stronger and stronger. I heard the glasses in the cupboards start shaking, and I felt the chairs slightly moving. I looked at my mom in fear, and she had an intense expression on her face that I couldn't read.

"Momma-" I began, but I was interrupted by a vigorous shake, knocking over Ness's chair and the glasses in the cupboards. Then I heard it. There was screaming, and laughter, and screeching. My mom grabbed me and my brother and rushed us upstairs and into the attic. I saw a glimpse of the outside as we ran up the stairs. There was blood. So much blood. I saw six men, they were laughing. They acted like demons, but they were so… handsome. They looked so trustworthy, yet they had blood on their hands, and people pleaded with them to stop. That's what scared me the most. I will never forget that. My mom shoved me and my brother, who was now crying, into an empty box. Tears began streaming down my face as my mother began taping the box shut.

"MOM WAI-" I began

"Don't shout. They'll hear you. I knew this day would come. It was inevitable."

"Wa-what do you mean??" I whimpered.

"Listen to me, Flynn, protect your brother, and remember love, stay true to yourself. I love you."

My mom paused in her tracks and turned back to me.

"Flynn, honey, never trust the man whose initials are D.W.."

And with that, she left me and my younger brother, Ness, who was four then. We spent two days in that box. I heard crying, begging, pleading, and laughter. Not a good laugh, though, no. A horrible, sadistic laughter. I woke up from that box after about 50 hours. At first, I thought I was dead; seeing how it is now, I wish that was the case. I felt a happy, angelic aura and saw a warm light.

"Do not be afraid, child, for I am your hope, your savior."

I heard the voice of an angel talking from outside the small box me and my brother were crammed in. I was so tired, hungry, and on the verge of death, and because of all this, I was quick to trust the voice that was calling out for me. Using my fingernails, I weakly cut open the box. I peeked my head out hesitantly; I froze in fear. The creature calling out to me looked like no angel, for it looked the closest to any demon I would've imagined, but then suddenly, I remembered the men I had seen from outside the window.

"Hello, my child, my name is Michael, and I come to help you."

I whimpered in fear. This man who had just offered me his help looked as if he'd be the last face I'd ever see. Yet, I felt safe around him, like I could trust him. He offered me his hand and explained what had happened in the last few days. Lucifer, with his army of sinners and fallen angels, had declared war against the angels, saints, and God. Lucifer would become more vital than ever with a machine made by humanity that converted energy into black magic. They called this machine *The Core*. With this new magic, he defeated the saints and God, banishing them to burn in Hell for all of eternity. With the bit of power the saints had left, they created a small place for the few remaining saints in Heaven, below where Lucifer now rules. It was the only place where sinners could not roam freely, creating chaos. This place was called the *Safe Haven*. Michael was God's strongest angel, enabling him to sneak underneath the Sinner's noses and help the remaining survivors.

"Do you trust me?"

Michael asked me.

I simply nodded, and he reached out to me. I took his hand while holding my brothers, and we were suddenly there. There were already tents, just a patch of grass and trees the size of a small neighborhood. I went over to an empty tent and gently placed Ness in it, allowing him to sleep. I looked behind me, and there was the barrier separating Safe Haven from Hell. Sinners were pounding on the barrier; they were throwing each other, trying to get to us, and then I saw them again. The same men I had seen before were there, waiting outside of the barrier. Many of them wore dull, stale expressions, except for one of them. He was wearing a smile. He looked so... Prideful? Like he was extremely cocky and proud of something. Beyond them, for as far as I could see, was blood, fire, and death everywhere, and I soon realized my mom was nowhere to be found. Outside the Safe Haven or inside it. Michael sensed my negative emotions and began speaking softly to me.

"Flynn, darling, why don't we get you some bread and wine?" Michael comforted me.

We headed to a small table with about 200 bread plates and red wine. I quickly scarfed down the plate and the wine. I grabbed an extra plate and drink for Ness and placed it alongside him. Michael explained how he had to get the remaining saints safely, and they'd be back soon. Before he left, he introduced me to an older gentleman known as *Mr. Evans*. Mr. Evans welcomed me to the small refuge and introduced me to the others. There were only 200 remaining saints in the world, and we only had the bare necessities; we had to farm and build homes and markets from scratch. We had no electricity, phones, or cars; we only had what God had given us in the first place: nature. After about a year and six months, with the help of our small community, we built our first house. It was small but sturdy. We soon realized that we saints could go in and out of the barrier but could only return if we did not allow our souls to be corrupted by the main tempting sins of Hell: Pride, Lust, Greed, Envy, Gluttony, Sloth and Wrath. If the saints stayed true to their beliefs and were not tempted by any of these sins, allowing their souls to remain pure, they could enter and leave the Safe Haven. If they allow their soul to become corrupted, they shall never be allowed to re-enter the Safe Haven again. Making them become just another sinner. **Back to the present day...**

I looked out the window and frowned. I wish things could just go back to the way they were. Now, it's a miracle if a child makes it to the 10th grade. Most kids just end up working once they turn twelve.

"Hey Flynn?" Ness asked.

"Yeah?"

"Do you think we'll ever make it out of here?"

I froze up when he asked me that question.

"Um, I don't know. Why do you ask?" I replied, looking back at him, a little startled.

"I don't know. I just- well... I just wish there was a hero, you know? Like someone who could go beyond the barrier without corrupting their soul, Like the stories you told me about that angle, Michael! Someone like him, someone like an angel. Someone strong."

I thought about this a lot, too. Of course, many people have tried to stop this madness and go beyond the barrier. If they were strong enough to make it through the violent and blood-hungry sinners, they'd be faced with the fallen angels. Many may be tempted by greed, lust, sloth, or pride, forgetting their beliefs and allowing themselves and their souls to be corrupted. Or at least that's what we've heard. Everyone who has tried to go beyond the barrier and destroy the machine that started this living hell had failed, leaving little to no hope for the Safe Haven. I hated seeing our community in shambles like this. There was barely enough food or water to go around. Before my mother died, she would always tell me to be brave, you know, cheesy stuff like that, but now I am starting to think what she said may be actual... She would want me to go out and destroy the machine that caused all this; she'd want me to be brave, wouldn't she? How would I do it, though? Maybe I'd bring a blessed weapon, perhaps just a prayer, maybe all I could carry with me is hope? ~~I couldn't be the hero.~~ *I could be <u>the hero.</u>*

My thoughts were interrupted by Ness asking me where to put the strawberries.

"Um, in the icehouse, you know that, buddy," I replied, a little shaken up.

Ness simply nodded and skipped out of the house.

I sat down at the kitchen table, put my face in the palms of my hands, and sighed. Did I want to venture out of the barrier? Well, of course, I did. Ever since my mother passed on, I wanted to stop this, to put an end to all of this, to avenge my mother, maybe, or to help my brother and his future. I don't know the exact reason, but I know I had to do it. Everything I had in me had to go into this. Oh, and about Ness. I could never bring him with me. I wouldn't be able to forgive myself if I brought him with me and something were to happen. I know I could leave him with our neighbor, Mr. Evan's. He wouldn't even question it; he'd take him in right away, allowing me to venture off into the land of the sinners. But what would Ness think? Would he support, accept, or tolerate this bizarre quest? Or would he nix, decline, or reject this adventure? Would he cry at the thought of me leaving? Maybe he'd celebrate it. My thoughts were once again interrupted by Ness.

"Flynn, I'm going to play with my friends at the farm; I'll be back for bedtime!"

"Oh, okay, buddy," I replied with a soft smile. Ness gave me a quick hug and ran out to play. I sighed and went over to my bed, and by bed, I mean a few logs, some hay, a cotton blanket, and a wool pillow. I tried to get the idea of leaving out of my head, but it didn't want to budge for some reason. It almost felt like someone, somewhere, needed me to do this. Maybe it was fate; perhaps it was my mom, who knows. I decided just to try to go to bed, like, hey, wanna escape from reality? Go to bed! It only took a few minutes before I drifted off into sleep.

I was suddenly awoken by a bright light as if someone were shining a flashlight into my eyes, but I knew that wasn't it; man, we didn't even have gas-powered lights. I squinted my eyes and tried to look away from the light, but it was as if no matter where I looked, it was there. Unexpectedly, I heard a voice.

"Come hither, and fear not, my child."

I should've been scared, but something about the voice and light was so comforting. I could hear the voice loud and clear, yet it sounded as if it came from inside my head. Without thinking, I stood up, allowing the light to consume me. The light suddenly became bearable to look at, which was odd considering that the brightness hadn't changed; it just now felt comfortable. The voice spoke yet again.

"My child, I have seen thee, and I have chosen thee to be the one who shall vanquish Lucifer and his host of sinners. As thy God, thou must hearken unto My voice. Go forth beyond the bounds that shelter thee, and conquer Lucifer by guarding thy soul from the stain of sin. Thou shalt shatter the device of the Evil One, that I and My angels may restore peace upon the earth. I trust in thee, Flynn, and I shall be with thee all thy journey long."

After the voice had said that, it had disappeared, and suddenly, I woke up. I jumped up in bed, sweating and breathing heavily. I knew what had just happened, but simultaneously, I was unsure of what had happened. I had met God, but was it just a dream? I couldn't shake the burning feeling that it wasn't, and now the idea of venturing out past the barrier felt even more appealing. I now knew what my purpose here on Earth was.

In the midst of my thoughts, I was suddenly interrupted by the voice of my brother, and I noticed it was dark out. How long had I been asleep?

"Hey Flynn! What are we going to have for dinner?"

What will I tell him?

What will he think?

Will he be okay with it?

Will he-

"Umm, hey, haha... Umm, some cabbage and apples. You know, ha, normal stuff."

Ness frowned, "what is it, Flynn?"

I laughed awkwardly, "W-what do you mean?"

"I know somethings wrong, Flynn; tell me what it is."

I found my mouth agape at the fact Ness could read my expression so easily.

"I-I don't know what you mean, Ness ahah- say umm, will you help me with dinner?"

Ness's stern face began to break, and tears streamed down his cheeks. I jumped up and panicked, rushing to his side.

"H-Hey Ness! What's wrong?!"

Ness started calming himself down as I pulled him into a tight embrace.

"I-I... Um-m,, I-I jus-st..." Ness whimpered.

"Hey buddy, look at me," Ness tilted his face slightly upwards to meet my gaze. "It's okay. Calm down and tell me what's bothering you."

Ness started speaking again, "I just... I—... I just don't want you to hide secrets from me. I know something's wrong, and you won't tell me. I'm your brother. I have a right to know."

My younger brother's words took me aback. He sounded so mature, and it scared me, but he was right. He does have a right to know. Ever since Mom died, I'd taken on too much of a parental role when, in truth, he is only five years younger than me.

I took a deep breath and began to explain myself.

"Okay, Ness, you got me. You're right, you do have a right to know, well…"

I took another deep breath.

"Okay," I began, "I have an idea. What if I crossed the barrier?"

Ness's jaw dropped, and he stammered backward, "W-what?"

"I know it sounds like a suicide mission, but just think, if I'm able to get to the Core and destroy it, we'll be free!"

"No, Flynn, you aren't thinking! Think about it: no one comes back after leaving the Safe Haven; what do you think will happen to you..?!"

"I will stay strong! You know I would! If I could just destroy the Core-!"

I was interrupted by Ness's yelling.

"AND WHAT IF YOU CAN'T DESTROY IT?! WHAT HAPPENS THEN? WHAT IF YOU END UP LIKE THAT GIRL, MILLIE?! W-what if... You don't even make it past the sinners? What about me? What would happen to *me, Flynn*? Please don't leave me like mom did."

I was astounded by Ness's sudden words. Part of me wanted to shout back, another wanted to cry, and another wanted just to give up, but I couldn't do any of those things because Ness ran out of the house, his eyes puffy and his nose red before I could even say anything. So I stood there, a fool, not able to move a single limb. I just... *dissociated.*

After a while, I finally re-collected myself. I walked over to the bathroom to wash my face with my bucket of water. I knew I should look for Ness to talk to him, but I couldn't bring myself to do so for some reason. I think... I just needed some time to cool off before any further interaction.

An hour passed before I tore myself from the chair I was sitting on to search for Ness.

Maybe he's right, I thought, *he needs me, I can't just leave him. I understand if he still needs me.*

After ten minutes of walking around, I found him. He was sitting underneath an old oak tree, playing with the floor around his feet. I walked up to him and sat beside him without saying anything. Before I could talk to him, he spoke to me first.

"I understand why you need to leave."

"And I understand why you don't want me to leave."

"No," Ness began, looking at me, "You need to go, and you know why, too. I trust that you won't make any stupid mistakes; I trust you, Flynn."

I didn't reply. I simply looked down at the flowers. It was a bittersweet feeling, really. Ness knew I needed to leave, and I did, too. Of course, it's not a choice I'd like to make, but we both acknowledged that this had to be done.

"So, Flynn, please," Ness whimpered, "please, go."

I nodded and got back up and onto my feet. I began to walk away but felt a tug on my pants.

"Please, Flynn, promise me you'll come back," Ness said, tears forming in his eyes.

That's when my expression broke. I felt tears begin to flow down the sides of my face.

"I promise, Ness. God, I promise." We embraced each other tightly and walked towards our neighbor's house, Mr. Evans. If someone were going to be watching Ness, it'd be him. Once we got to Mr. Evans's house, we explained what was happening and asked if he could watch Ness while I was gone. Mr. Evans made me promise not to do anything stupid before saying goodbye and taking Ness by the hand. Before walking away, Ness and I shared a final embrace and said our goodbyes.

Before leaving the barrier, it's a custom to be blessed by a pastor, along with any items you may take on your journey. I packed bread and water for about two weeks and an old dagger my mother gifted on my 8th birthday. It had rubies all along it, as sharp as a needle. A beautiful thing, really. After my objects and I were blessed by the pastor, along with a final prayer for my protection, he showed me to the gate. The gate was in the church, alongside a mural of angels. Outside the gate, I saw just red. I saw blood everywhere, fire, and dried ground, but no demons or sinners in sight. The pastor gave me one last option: to back out, and once I said no, he opened the gate for me.

This is it; this is my destiny. ***I will be their savior.***

Somewhere in the Core...

"Sir!" A demon rushed in.

"What is it, you filth?"

"A saint has crossed the barrier!"

"And? Just let the sinner take a bite out of it; problem solved."

"No, this saint is... **different**. There seems to be something about it. Like as if there was a stronger angel or saint protecting them."

"No... You must be mistaken. It isn't possible... Right?"

"It seems to be, sir. I believe this saint will cause a problem in the long run."

"Ugh." A third voice steeped in, "Do not worry, son, for this shall not be a problem." He touched the other man's shoulder and turned to the demon, "If you truly believe there is reason for concern, do not worry; I have just the girl."

"Are you saying...?"

"Yes. Tell **Lilith** she has a new play toy..."

Chapter Two

An hour has passed since I left the barrier. I needed to make my way to Earth since Safe Haven was placed in Heaven, just as Lucifer ruled; it would take about two days to get back to Earth. I'd have to take the stairway to Heaven; well, the proper term would now be the stairway to Hell.

It didn't take too long until I encountered my first battle. It was two sinners, most likely tempted by lust or *Asmodeus*. The funny thing about sinners who were originally people or saints is that they carry characteristics from when they were alive/saints, and you can quickly tell what sin made them sinners by how they act. For example, these sinners had wandering eyes, and they had a particular look in their eyes that showed they craved lust. I was walking along a vast area of dead bushes, and they jumped at me, attempting to grab my neck, but I jumped backward before they could. They hissed and snarled at me before jumping at my fingers, just able to nick me. I pulled my hand back in pain, and one started cackling. I swiftly pulled my blessed dagger from my pocket and swung at their stomachs, hitting one. The one I swung at hissed in pain, and the other jumped towards the dagger I was yielding. As it jumped closer to me, I plunged the dagger into its throat and watched it freeze and then turn to dust. The other attempted to bolt away, but I threw my dagger at it, hitting it in the back of the head. My dagger dropped from its head as it turned to dust, and I fell to my knees.

I contemplated going back. I wondered if this journey would be too much for me. I felt a weird pit in my stomach, knowing those sinners were once people like me, and now they were solely dust. When I was younger, I remember reading books and watching movies where the hero killed the villains, and they never felt *like this*. I felt as if I could throw up.

~~I am too weak for this.~~ **_I will get stronger._**

I pulled myself up from my knees and grabbed my dagger. I still felt a pit in my stomach, like butterflies in my stomach, but instead of them fluttering around innocently, they were stabbing me; the pit was easier to deal with now as I kept repeating affirmations in my head. I swallowed the lump in my throat as I looked at the dust my dagger and I had caused.

I continued walking through Hell in the sky until I finally reached the staircase that led down to Earth, where I knew the Core had to be due to that being the demos' main entrance point. The staircase was not like the one you'd imagine, like a beautiful white pristine staircase. Oh no, no, no, no… It was hot, hot like magma, with dust and ashes all over it. The handrail was not beautiful; thorns were twisting and invading the once beautiful handrail. I began to make my way down the staircase that seemed to go on forever slowly, but then, once I realized the heat was melting the soles of my shoes, I began to hop and run down the stairs.

One fall…

I thought,

One fall, and it's all over.

I began to lose my balance, I swore, I started falling.

Then… that's when I heard it.

I heard a voice, a beautiful, angelic voice,

"Do not be afraid, my child," it began, *"For I will protect thee; thy journey shall **not** be cut short by clumsiness."*

Then I was at the bottom of the stairs.

It was like a fever dream, one moment falling to my demise and the next, on my feet, not a scratch in sight. I checked my hand where the previous sinner had cut me, and there was no longer a cut. I quickly cupped my hand over my mouth to avoid gasping as a droplet of sweat fell down the side of my face. I looked back up to the staircase, and I swear, just for a moment, I saw the figure of a man looking down at me at the higher steps of the stairs just before vanishing into thin air. I froze for a second before I was brought back to reality by a loud crashing noise.

I looked towards where I had heard the noise, and I suddenly felt extremely hot, as if a fire surrounded me. I felt as if I were going to pass out, and before I could do anything about it, I began to feel my eyelids get heavier and heavier until finally… I closed them.

...

I began to open my eyes slowly and hesitantly. I checked the bag in which I had all my supplies, and I luckily still had all my food and water in it, but there was something missing, which happened to be my dagger. I began to observe my surroundings, and it seemed that I was lying in the middle of a circle, *a circle with a star in the middle.* I quickly hopped to my feet and stumbled back. I was lying in the middle of a pentagram, and at each corner of the star, there were candles. A wave of fear and distress hit me as I noticed there was nothing but a few desolate trees and a few bushes, and I was no longer anywhere near the staircase.

I heard a giggle from behind me. I turned around swiftly and looked to where I had listened to the laughter. It was a girl. She seemed to have no eyes, patchy, dry skin, and dark, silky hair that reached past her shoulders. She had a pasty white skin tone and a sinister smile plastered onto her face. She was spinning my dagger at her fingertips.

"So you're the boy everyone's making a fuss about.." The girl stated.

"D-DON'T COME ANY C-CLOSER!" I shouted in response.

She didn't speak back to me or even flinch; she simply laughed. She tried to hide it, but I could tell she was inspecting me, most likely seeing if I had a weapon.

*"I'd say... They're wrong about you, young man... I think- aha! I think you're **weak**."*

With that being said, she lunged at me.

I stumbled backward, but I was too late. She sat on top of my chest, restricting any movements I could make. I began writhing in pain, attempting to break her grip on me. But she didn't budge. Seeing my attempt at escaping her painful hold, she started laughing, and with each movement I made, it only grew more and more frenetic. I tried scratching her, punching her, biting her, but she didn't even flinch. I knew I stood no chance, but I couldn't go down without a fight. I just kept thinking of the promise I made to my brother the very same day, the promise that I would return, that I would see him again. It all seemed hopeless now.

Eventually, she held my very same dagger above her head, reading to plunge it into my fragile skin any minute now. All I could think of doing was praying. Pray for my safety, pray for my brother, pray for the freedom of all saints, pray for my friends, my neighbors. Pray for everyone. I began seeing the girl wiggle the dagger around in her hands, laughing wildly. I squeezed my eyes shut, preparing myself for the sudden pain I'd feel, but I only felt her grip loosen. I opened my eyes and saw her looking quizzically at the trees. I used this opportunity to push her off of me. Using all my force, I pushed her off of me, and she hit the ground within no time. She looked at me, first looking surprised, then her eyes filled with rage, and her lips curved into a smile.

"That was a mistake, pretty boy." She smiled, preparing herself to attack me once again.

Before she could run at me and swing, Another jumped out from behind a nearby tree, catching the attention of me and the girl who had me on the brink of death. The more petite girl who just ran out from the tree didn't look to be much older than me, maybe a year or two? I seemed to recognize her, but I couldn't quite put my finger on it.

Before I knew it, the girl began reciting ancient words out loud, and a wall of white light shot into the other girl's arm. The girl who was just recently attacking me winced in pain, and her arm bag boiled. The beam of light also hit me, but it did nothing to my skin as it had done to the other girl.

The girl held her arm, hissed, and quickly ran away in pain

"YEAH QUOD IUSTUM FUGIENDUM SARCULO!" The girl shouted after the girl ran away, "SCRAM DAEMONIUM!" I looked at the girl, puzzled, wondering what she was saying. "Salve?" The girl continued, "Non loqueris?" I again looked at her with a confused expression.

"Ummm," the girl started, "d-do you speak English."

I nodded quickly at her.

"Ohhhh! Ha! Sorry about that! I thought you were a sinner! So many sinners speak ancient languages, so I've been trying to catch up on some of them. I- wait... do I know you?"

We both began studying each other. We both obviously knew we knew each other, but both of us seemed to have trouble understanding exactly *where* we knew each other from.

"I- umm-" I began, "maybe did you live in LA..?"

"No," she replied, "I'm from Boston... Say, what's your name?" Maybe that will help me remember ahah-" She laughed awkwardly.

"Oh! Yeah, my name's Flynn."

"Wait... FLYNN?!" Her jaw dropped, "It's been some time, aye!"

"Umm, I am so sorry, but I- well, I don't exactly know who you are..?"

"Oh yeah! It's me, Millie! From Safe Haven? I, like, left only like a month ago."

I felt my eyes light up. Millie was one of the only people in Safe Haven who was around my age. We used to do everything together, from reading to just demon-watching. However, about two years ago, we stopped talking because I dropped out of school to work.

"Well, I'll be damned!" I exclaimed. "It really is you, Millie! You- I- I don't even know what to say! Just that- your appearance changed a lot!"

"Haha!" Millie laughed, "W-what do you mean.?"

"I- um- just like you look different, you know, since the last time we talked!"

"Oh! Yeah, hahaha- I understand!"

We both sat in silence for a moment until I broke the silence.

"So… how did you do that white light thing?"

"Oh, that thing I did to that demon girl?"

"Yeah."

"Oh, that was easy! It was just a simple protection prayer! I can teach you if you want!"

I thought about how she called it a *simple protection prayer*. It was definitely **not** simple. Thinking about it, it'd be a fantastic advantage to have against future enemies to know how to boil their skin at will, but knowing Millie, or at least *past* Millie, she'll want something in return.

"Yeah, that'd be awesome if you could teach me!"

"Okay, I got you, but only if you're willing to pay a price first."

I rolled my eyes, I saw this trap, but I still fell for it; this was on me.

"What do you want, Millie?"

She laughed, and her eyes began to drift off in a random direction.

"What is it, Millie?" I said, with a slight hint of concern in my voice.

She sighed and looked at me. "Flynn, I screwed up." Her voice began to break, "I screwed up big time... I- I'm going to die soon." She said, tears forming in her eyes, but she held a smile. Just like she always did.

"W-what do you mean, Millie.?"

"My soul is being corrupted.."

I began to worry a tremendous amount, "What do you want me to do, Millie…?"

She looked at me, visibly distraught, "I know you're going to try to destroy the Core... That's the only reason you'd leave your brother; I know that I just want you to. Well... If I teach you how to do what I did, I want you to bring me on your journey and make me useful before I die from this virus of a sin."

I didn't know what to say; Millie was always a cheerful, funny person. The type of person that makes you feel happy; now she was telling me about how she was going to die? I knew once again what I had to do; she was my crutches during my hard times back then, and now I can be hers.

"Of course, Millie," I reassured her, "I won't let you die alone."

She smiled at me and hugged me. We stayed like that for a few seconds before deciding to continue our journey, and before we knew it, we were off, *off to save the world.*

Somewhere in the Core…

The girl whined in pain as a demon began treating her boiling skin.

"Jesus Christ!" A voice rushed in, "What the hell happened! All he said to do was kill the boy! He is just a boy! How did you lose so easily!?"

"I d-don't know, dammit! He had another saint with him! A-a girl! Jesus, this burns like hell! She did some weird spell thing! God, I don't know! She landed a blow on me! And it hurt!"

The third ominous voice arose from the shadows, "Are you saying you are becoming… **weak,** darling?"

"N-no! And don't call me darling! I am **nothing** to you!" The girl hissed, looking away embarrassed.

"From the looks of it, love, you are becoming weak." He grabbed her hand where she had been burned and inspected it as she hissed in pain. "Ha," he laughed and grabbed her *chin, "**You are just as weak and worthless as you look.**" He threw her to the ground and began speaking to the other man or, as we know, the other voice, "tell Asmodeus that this* **filth** *of a woman couldn't even kill a child. Hopefully, he won't be as stupid as her. Tell him to do what he wants with them; as long as they are dead in the next 24 hours, I will be pleased."*

"Tell the demon to get him." He replied, in a cold tone, "I have more **important** matters to tend to. You know that, **Lucifer.**"

Chapter Three

As we continued walking to God knows, I began to ask Millie eagerly questions about how she had learned to recite those protection spells. In a way, I was so content with asking her questions to somewhat avoid the central conflict that she might die. Now, I say I might because deep down, I still had a feeling of denial. Of course, we weren't as close as we were before; God, you could even say the only thing I know about her right now was that she'd die, or so she says. I wanted to be close to her, even if we fell out years ago. I wanted to get to know her again, but I was scared she'd reject my interest in our newly found friendship. To be completely honest, I believe that she sensed how I was avoiding the topic of her passing, and I think she somewhat appreciated it.

There was one question I was dreading asking, which would be vital to our quest, and that question was if she knew where the *Core* was located. My plan was to go and destroy the Core, but in reality, I needed to find out where it was located.

"Hey, Millie?" I asked.

"Yeah?"

"I don't know if you know, but do you know where the Core is located?"

Millie looked at me, puzzled, and then began laughing.

"What.-?" I questioned.

"Y-you left the Safe Haven without even knowing where the Core is?!" Millie laughed.

I looked down at my feet, flustered. I guess it was an incredibly dumb idea, and now I hoped that this whole idea of mine wasn't just a fantasy like Ness had previously stated.

"I mean, I have an idea of where the Core is; I mean- I don't have the *exact* coordinates, but I do know how we know we are getting close and stuff."

I let out a relieved sigh, and Millie continued.

"I do know that we need just to keep walking East, knowing where that demon girl tried to kill you, and once we get closer, Hell begins to look more like a paradise rather than, well, you know, Hell." She smiles and pulls a compass out of her bag, "And don't worry, I have one of these bad boys, so we'll know where East is at all times! Another thing, though, is that the closer we get to the Core, we might encounter some of the other *Fallen Angels*. And that's precisely why we need to train you!"

"W-what?!" I exclaimed.

"Oh c'mon' Flynn, we both know you're not exactly the best fighter, and you could certainly use some work."

I rolled my eyes, mostly because I knew she was right. I wasn't the best soldier; that was one of my most significant flaws.

"So get up, soldier!" Millie jumped up, "let's get to work!"

That was the moment when my entire ego laid flat as a piece of paper. Millie and I worked on my combat skills for about 2 hours, and the more we went on, the worse I got and the better she got. Worst of all, every time I'd get tired or begin to sweat, insults flew directly at me and my now crushed and humbled ego, but I can say with confidence it did pay off.

Now, at least I can block punches and throw them properly, you know, without looking like I was just flaring my arms around. Soon, the muddy and sweaty weather began to cool down, but that's the funny part about this unique Hell. It's terribly hot during the day, but during the night, it's freezing cold. You could say it really adds personality to Hell, but I wish it didn't have any.

"Okay-" Millie sat down against a tree. "It's getting darker, so we should find shelter somewhere if we can, at least."

I groaned, "Thank God. I thought you were going to beat even more of the living Hell out of me."

Millie giggled and began to walk into the distance.

"Wait- Millie!" I yelled, "Where are you going?!"

"How'd you think I survived in this damn place for so long? C'mon', I know a good place to sleep."

I awkwardly did a fast-paced walk to catch up to Millie. Not too long after we began walking, our surroundings almost became unrecognizable due to it becoming dark and swift. I looked around nervously, trying to allow my eyes to focus on something, anything. To be honest, it was embarrassing to have to be trained because of my lack of physical combat and needing to be chauffeured around on foot because of how little I knew about this place. Eventually, I heard Millie's footsteps stop, and I held to a halt as a result.

"Here it is!" Millie exclaimed, "The best place to get the worst sleep you'll ever get!"

I heard Millie run into wherever this "shelter" was as if she had memorized the steps of where it was and how to get inside. Soon enough, I saw a faint glow coming from inside of a small opening in a mountain. I looked inside to see Millie and her knees, lightly lighting a small fire on a bundle of small sticks, using two thin sticks.

"Wow." I said, stepping into the small cave, "This isn't too bad."

"Right!" Millie jumped up from the fire and threw the two sticks she was using to light the fire into the fireplace. "It's not exactly the comfiest place to sleep, but hey! It's better than nothing. Please tell me you brought a sleeping bag or pillow of some sort because I'm used to sleeping here now, but it'll be very uncomfortable for you since it's your first time sleeping here."

"Oh please," I began cockily, "I may not have a pillow or sleeping bag, but I slept in a literal cardboard box for days with my brother. I think I can handle a rough floor."

Millie sighed and lay on the ground. "Whatever you say, dude. Anyway, try to get some sleep now; we have a long day tomorrow, so I will have to walk more to where I think the core is. Goodnight."

I got myself situated and laid on the ground, "okay. Goodnight, Millie."

All I can say about that night is that I shouldn't have been so arrogant about sleeping on the ground because I never slept worse than that night in my whole life. I don't know what the floor in Hell is made up of, but I've never felt a more uncomfortable, hard floor. After straight hours of twisting, turning, staring at the ceiling, and watching Millie sleep so soundly as if she were sleeping on a cloud, I was finally able to get some sleep. That night, I dreamt of the man I saw on the stairs when I had almost tripped down. He spoke to me, a warning.

"Flynn," the bright silhouette approached me. I looked around; there was nothing for miles. All I could see was bright white as if no matter how far I'd go, I would not be able to leave. I attempted to talk, only to begin panicking once I noticed I couldn't speak like I had no tongue. "Do not be afraid, my child," the bright light continued, "for I have come with advice for the next challenge you shall face. To beat this, you mustn't allow yourself to be tempted by lust, for *Asmodeus* will attempt to pursue you with his many attractions. Just remember, my child, if your right eye causes you to stumble, gouge it out and throw it away. It is better to lose one part of your body than for your whole. If your right hand causes you to stumble, cut it off and throw it away because it is better to lose one part of your body than your whole. Stay true to your moral values; do not allow your lust to get in the way. For even one peek at those women, you've already lost. If you must resort to alternate ways to eliminate him, he and his army are quite easy to fool. Just be smarter, and I trust you will be, my son."

Before I could even react, I began to fall. I wanted to scream, but I couldn't. I fell through the floor, and I saw the white dream room I was once in begin to bleed black. The dark colors consumed the light until I could only see the white figure, but it felt as if I was staring through water because the figure began to distort until I could no longer see it. Soon, I began to feel extremely hot, and then I saw myself. I was sleeping, and I was sweating profusely. I kept falling until I fell perfectly into my own body, and I was then back into my body. I jolted forward, confused, and started. I wiped the sweat from my face as I slowly began recollecting my thoughts. I looked around the small cave. It was "morning," so basically, it was scorching. The fire was out, and I cupped my head in my hands.

"Millie?" I called out.

There was no answer.

I looked to where Millie should've been. She wasn't there.

I called her name again, now panicking. I quickly jumped up to my feet and ventured outside the cave, still calling out her name. I began slowly recognizing my surroundings. There were trees, trees with actual leaves, which was a surprise for Hell, knowing that the trees were usually burnt to the crisp. I noticed that that was the reason I kept hearing the sounds of leaves; at the moment, I thought I was only imagining it. I continued going farther away from the cave, still searching. I was now fully hyperventilating. I kept imagining the worst thing that could've happened to her, like what if she was attacked? Ambushed? But all I had was hope, so I kept searching.

"Millie?!" I shouted.

Finally, I found her. I gasped and ran up to her, but she showed no emotion whatsoever. She just looked *numb*.

"Jeez, Millie! You scared me half to death!" I exclaimed, now sitting on the ground beside her.

"Oh," Millie began, "I'm sorry, I just don't actually know why I'm out here really; I was just looking at the view."

She looked out in front of her, and I followed her gaze. I didn't notice at first, but she was sitting on the ledge of a cliff. It was a beautiful view, really. The sky was a pretty golden and pinkish color. There was a dried-up river, cracked at its base. It was a really, really lovely sight, knowing we were in Hell.

"So-" I started, "why are you over here really?"

Millie just shrugged and continued staring blankly at the horizon, so I just kept her company and sat by her in silence. A few moments passed before Millie spoke.

"I don't know if you ever told me, but where were you during the first day Hell broke loose? Were you with your family?"

"Oh. Yeah, um, I don't think I've ever told you. I was with my brother. We were hiding in a box my mom taped shut for a few days."

Millie's head perked up. "Do you know where your mom is now?"

I looked away and shook my head. We continued sitting in silence for a moment until I finally broke the silence.

"What about you?"

Millie looked away for a second and then started talking. "I was hiding with my baby niece. I was babysitting her, and then it began, you know. We hid under a bed, and she kept crying. I heard some people, probably the sinners, come into the room. She kept freaking crying, and I was only ten. I didn't know what to do, so I pushed her out from under the bed."

Millie looked away and stopped talking, not finishing the story, but I already knew what happened after that. Those sinners were cramped up in Hell for so long; they were crazy and blood-hungry like they are nowadays, too. Eventually, Millie got up and grabbed my hand to pull me up as well.

"Well, we can't let our stupid backstories get in the way of us saving the world, can we?"

I smiled and nodded, and we went back to the cave to grab my bag. After I got my stuff, we got on our way, using solely our hope and hopefully any higher power to lead us in the right direction. We walked and walked until I swore we were getting nowhere. Then, we started hearing club music and seeing spotlights or various colors. As we followed the sounds, I started seeing beautiful fruit trees, green grass, cars, and even beautiful pavement. Once we finally got to where all the noise and lights were coming from, we saw people. Beautiful people. The place reeked of alcohol, cheap perfume, and cologne. The people who were standing outside of the building had very unrealistic model-type bodies. The women wore short, tight dresses, mini skirts, and some even in bras. The men were almost all shirtless; the ones who wore shirts were very tight-fitting, and most of them also wore tight-fitting jeans or trousers.

Then I remembered what the man in my dream had told me.

"Millie," I whispered, "try not to allow the lust to overtake you. Try to stay pure; we just have to have a stronger mentality. I had a dream just about this."

Millie chuckled, "Trust me, it won't matter for me."

We both began approaching the entrance to the building. The building had lovely architecture, neon lights all around it, and the title of the building. The title read,

Asmodeus Night Club

As soon as I read the title, the atmosphere changed. I looked all around me, and it looked like Earth before the demons purged it. It became darker, and a moon lingered overhead. Though at first glance it looked like a Vegas strip, it began looking faker and faker. Soon, a car pulled up to the club; it was a nicely dressed man with a husky voice and light blue eyes. His vehicle was quickly swarmed with men and women.

"Ladies, gentlemen, please. I know you all would like me, but you need to wait your turn, darlings."

The people stood back from his car door, and the door swung open. He wore an expensive *Rolex*-type watch, and his hands were veiny and strong-looking. Even though he wore a looser suit, you could still tell he was very muscular.

His eyes darted around where he was for a second until his eyes met mine and Millie's. I watched the corners of his mouth slowly rise into a smile, and he looked as if he wanted to approach us. Millie noticed it as well, and she looked flustered and straightened up. At first, he attempted to just walk over to us, but he was unsuccessful because the crowd of people was still swarming him. He looked almost mad, so he began pushing his way out of the crowd. Men and women fell onto each other due to being shoved, and soon, he made his way to us.

"Hello, you two." He greeted us, smiling. "Aren't you two a little too young to be at a club?"

Millie and I said nothing, and we both glanced at one another.

"Oh, it's okay, I won't tattle-tell on you. Honestly, it's been a while since younger adults came here."

Millie and I still haven't said a word.

"Why now, I don't bite." He said, chuckling. "My name's Asmodeus and you two are?"

"U-um-" Millie hesitated. "I- I'm Millie-"

"What a beautiful name for a beautiful lady." Asmodeus winked and grabbed her hand, leaning down to kiss it in a gentleman-like way. "And you are?" He gestured to me, smirking.

"Uh- I'm Flynn," I replied, sticking my hand out to shake him awkwardly.

"What a gentleman you are, Flynn." He looked me up and down, shaking my hand. "Let me show you two inside! I'm sure *you'll love it*."

Chapter Four

"Ahh, here we are!" Asmodeus exclaimed as we entered the club. As soon as we all entered, the building seemed to stretch, as if the building we saw outside was merely a decoy. As we walked, we began to take notice of all the minute details and soon realized there wasn't any door out except for the one we had entered.

Looking around, there were many little symbols of the Devil, such as goat heads, snakes, and even stars in circles. These little designs were so well hidden that if you weren't searching for them, you would've never noticed they were there.

Often, I felt eyes watching me, and when I glanced up, I saw the purple glow from Asmodeus's eyes meet mine. It was evident that he was studying me and Millie, maybe trying to read us? The second we would make eye contact, his mouth would contort into a wide grin, flashing me his sharp white teeth. I would immediately look away, intimidated by the evil gaze in his eyes.

"See anything you like, Flynn?" Asmodeus remarked, speaking through his smile.

"Uhm-" I blushed awkwardly and looked to Millie for guidance, just to see her very intrigued by everything that was going on around us. "I can't say I do, uh, sir. I'm not really uhm- into this kind of thing." I say, trying to avoid eye contact nervously.

"Oh, nothing? Why must there be *something* that you like here? What do you find sexy, Flynny?"

As soon as Asmodeus called me by that name, I visibly cringed and took a deep breath, embarrassed on his behalf.

"I uh- I don't really see people like that- sorry- I'm the wrong guy to ask." I stood up straight and said this, sticking out my chest, trying to look confident, but my hand tightly gripping the strap of my bag gave away my nervousness. Asmodeus saw this, and his sinister smile only grew. He looked over at Millie, who was admiring the decor and watching the people in the club. They were drinking and, well, baby-making. C'mon', what were we expecting? It's Asmodeus.

"Uhm-" I began, "why don't you uh- ask Millie? I'm not the right person to ask about that stuff."

Asmodeus looked over at Millie, studying her for a minute. His eyes flickered with disappointment, and his smile softly faded before looking back at me, his grin widening. "Well, your little girlfriend seems to, well, already have accepted sin. You, however, haven't." He looked me up and down, studying me. "I want to see that happen, pretty boy." I looked over to Millie, who was still intrigued by the things that were happening around the two of us. Asmodeus continues to stare at me; even after I stop speaking and break our eye contact, he still shows his wide grin and watches my every move. "Well," Asmodeus begins. "I may have an idea of what you might like." He mentions over to Millie and grins.

With that grin, he shoves me and Millie into a room that I hadn't noticed prior to being shoved in. I tried to get out of the room, but I was too late. Asmodeus flashed me a sinister smile and closed the door, locking it. "Have fun, you two!" He teased, and then his footsteps were heard receding from the door.

I studied the room and realized it was a dimmed bedroom with a large bed and candles on a nightstand. I looked back at Millie and saw her studying the room as well, looking visibly uncomfortable. I tried to open the door, but it was locked from the outside. This made me even more anxious, and I began hyperventilating.

"Hey, dude, look at me; we'll be okay," Millie said comfortingly, grabbing my shoulders and forcing me to look at her. "We're gonna get out of here; it'll all be okay." I looked into her eyes and nodded. "Yeah," I began, "you're right." Millie's words calmed me down a bit, but I was still fidgeting with my bag and hands.
"Man, though," Millie sighed, "he really is enticing. He's my literal ideal type."

"Huh? What do you mean?" I questioned.

"Dude, he has, like, everything I look for in a guy. Blue eyes, black hair, a nice cologne."

"What? He doesn't have cologne; he has green eyes and blonde hair. That's weird; he looks different to me than you." I shrug my shoulders.

Millie shrugs and looks around the room. She starts opening the drawers of the nightstands next to the bed, looking for something.

"What are you doing?" I say, moving closer to her to watch what she is doing.

"Looking for something. There might be something here to help us out." Millie opens a drawer and pulls out a bag of hair supplies, smiling. "Glad they thought about me looking good before doing you, huh?" She smirked and teased and went to the door, taking a hair clip and inserting it into the keyhole.

"Are you- are you pick locking the door?" I ask, intrigued.

"Yep!" Millie smiles and continues to work the door. "My parents were poor, so let's just say they had a creative way of getting money. Besides, we've spent enough time here. We need to get to the core."

"Yeah, you're right, but what? I mean, I knew you were poor, but I didn't know your parents were criminals."

"Hey! They weren't criminals, dude." Millie hissed, not making eye contact. "Not everyone had your perfect little Californian life, okay."

"Millie, I wasn't trying to imply anything, I-" I sighed. "I was just saying. They were criminals. I'm sure there had to be a better way to go about money, though. What about the people they stole from?" I cross my arms and roll my eyes.

"Omg my god, Flynn, just drop it, damn. I don't care about what you think about my parents; you didn't have to worry about money because of your stupid, happy, rich family life. I didn't have that. I had to work." Millie grunts and continues to fidget with the door until we both hear a click, and she stands up and faces me. "I don't know why I'm telling you this anyway; we don't have time to argue. We have to go."

I sighed but nodded. Millie began to open the door, but I stopped her. "Wait, we need a plan. We can't just go in there blind."

Millie nodded and shut the door, "okay then, what's your plan."

"Well, I don't exactly have everything thought out, but I was thinking we could book it to the exit. It should be a straight shot from here."

Millie scoffed and raised an eyebrow, "that's your plan?"

"You have a better one?" I quickly commented. At this, Millie just sighed and nodded. Seeing this, I smiled and nodded back, giving her the okay to open the door.

Millie and I slowly opened the door and tried to run out, but Asmodeus was awaiting us outside the bedroom room, with a sinister smile and a purple, pinkish glow in his eyes.

"Leaving so soon? But you haven't gotten a taste of what my lovely establishment has to offer!" Asmodeus smiles widely, his grin becoming harder to look at.

"Yeah, man, uhm, what Flynn said." Millie started, "We aren't interested in what you have to offer, so we're going to leave. Thanks for uh- what you did." Millie says sternly, trying to move past him, but is stopped by Asmodeus putting an arm in front of her.

"Oh dear, not so soon. You haven't even had a drink!" Asmodeus snaps his fingers, and a drink is summoned into his hand. Even standing feet away, I could tell how strong it reeked of alcohol. Asmodeus held the drink out to Millie, who shook her head in disgust. He then held the drink up to my face, where I pushed it away from me.

"No thanks. Now, if you don't mind, we're going to leave." I say sternly.

Asmodeus sees how determined Millie and I are to leave, and his grin just spreads, but this time, his grin is so vast the skin at the corners of his mouth begins to tear, revealing his muscles. Millie and I stare in horror as his grin continues to expand, and more and more of his skin stretches to the point of tearing. Asmodeus laughs through his teeth and speaks in a sinister voice.

"What made you think you had a choice?"

After Asmodeus said this, his arms began to snap loudly, and his body was contorted. His arms were being snapped in half, and we could see his bones and the blood and bruises forming at the fractures. Millie and I could just stare in shock as Asmodeus's body continued to break and bend and stretch, all while his sinister smile grew, and he laughed maniacally.

Soon, the bruises from where his bones broke were slowly replaced with black fur, and the fur only spread from there. Soon, blood was spilling everywhere on the ground, and Millie began to stumble back as her shoes became engulfed in blood. I couldn't move. Soon, all we could see was blood, but suddenly, there was a change. The fur had replaced all of his skin but his head. He now had hooves for feet, much like a sheep, but hands much like a human. Even though he was facing towards us, behind him, you could hear a soft hissing sound. *He had a tail of serpents.* I could only stare as his face began to split in two, and three heads grew in place. The first one was a bull, then a man, and lastly, a goat. Even after all of this, his chilling smile remained.

Finally, I awoke from my standing coma when I heard Millie shout for me.

"FLYNN! MAKE A RUN FOR THE DOOR!"

Suddenly, I was aware of my surroundings again. I looked ahead of me and saw a small opening that I could use to bolt for the door. I ran at full speed past Asmodeus, and Millie followed. As we ran, I looked around to see the other people of the club scream violently as their bodies melted and were replaced with the body of a demon, except their traits were far more defined, leaving a much more terrifying demon than what is found at the beginning of Hell.

As Millie and I ran, the room seemed to stretch. No matter how fast we ran, we made no progress. The room just continued to pull. "What the hell!?" Millie yelled desperately and was out of breath. Shortly after, I heard a loud, bone-chilling scream. The scream sounded like a man, but there was also the sound of a bull and ram. I then heard footsteps. Then the footsteps got faster and louder, and soon, it was full-on running. I looked back. I shouldn't have looked back. There he was, Asmodeus, running on all fours, all of his heads screaming the faster he ran. Tears began forming in my eyes.

"This is the end. This is the end. This is the end."

All I could think about was why I went on this dumb quest, to begin with. I had a feeling? I thought I was fit? No, I was dumb. Soon, my thoughts went to Ness. Ness... Ness needed me. I couldn't let it end like this. With the bit of courage I had left, I took a look around and thought of a new plan.

"Millie!" I yelled to Millie, as she was a little ahead of me. "Go left into that room! We need to hide!"

"You better not let this fail!" Millie yelled and took a quick turn to the right. This threw me off, but I followed regardless. Soon, we found a small bar and hid at the bottom of it. We tried to keep our cries quiet and breathing low as we heard the footsteps of Asmodeus, and soon, we began hearing the familiar noises of the sinner, their moaning as they searched for us as well. After what seemed an eternity, we heard footsteps follow into a hallway away from us. Millie and I let out a deep breath, and I finally recuperated and thought of a plan.

"Okay, okay, we really need to get out of here," I said quietly but frantically, and Millie nodded in agreement. "Okay, this is what we have to do." I pull out my blessed dagger. "I will attack Asmodeus, but you need to get him alone. I need you to distract the other demons."

"What?" Millie asked, looking shocked. "Okay, dude, but how? I don't have a blessed dagger or anything!"

"Millie!" Flynn half whispers, "Did you just forget all those awesome spells and incantations? Lure them away with a spell!"

Suddenly, Millie's eyes glimmer with hope, and she smiles and nods. "Honestly, that might be the best idea you've had yet." She teased and then took a deep breath, "Let's do this." As soon as I heard this, I smiled and nodded, and we both emerged from our hiding spot. I was tightly gripping my dagger, and Millie was whispering under her breath, preparing herself for the cantation she'd use. As soon as we stepped out from under the bar, demons immediately turned to face us, and Asmodeus was seen staring at the two of us from across the room. Predictably, the demons rushed at Millie and me, and Millie began her incantation to lure them away.

"Sequeris me, quia tentatio sum. Sequimini me filii mei, ut vos ad veram huius mundi lucem perducam."

With those words, the demons all turned to face Millie, and then she ran. The demons chased and followed as Millie ran out of the room, and I was left alone with Asmodeus.

I turned to face the price of Hell before me, looking him in the eyes as I prepared myself for battle. I watched as his sinister grin grew seeing me, and all 3 of his heads fixated on me. He did not say a word, yet I could hear his sinister chuckling through his permanent smile. I took a deep breath and ran at him. He smiled and used his tail to fling me back, and I banged against the wall. This wouldn't stop me. I got back up and ran towards him again. He swung his tail towards me, yet this time, I ducked and sliced his leg, causing him to let out a shriek. Seeing this as an opportunity, I climbed onto his back and plunged my dagger straight into one of his three heads, his human head.

I tried to go for the other two heads, but I was pulled off by his serpent tail and flung back against the ground. I saw as the blood from his man's head dripped slowly down his body, but the blood was not red, unlike the time he transformed; it was black now. Asmodeus continued to use his tail to fling me around the room. I hit wall after wall after wall. I was hurt, and he was too strong to face alone. I needed help.

Just then, I remembered the actual person that I was helping by doing this quest. I took a deep breath, and I began to recite all the bible verses that I could remember regarding lust. This was my hopeful attempt at weakening him. Even if the sinners have infiltrated the universe, the saints must still weaken them in some way, right? So I began.

"PUT TO DEATH, THEREFORE, WHATEVER BELONGS TO YOUR EARTHLY NATURE: SEXUAL IMMORALITY, IMPURITY, LUST, EVIL DESIRES AND GREED, WHICH IS IDOLATRY, COLOSSIANS 3:5!"

I shouted this with such confidence it urged me to keep going. I saw Asmodeus wince in pain after my recital, which only gave me more confidence.

"IF YOUR RIGHT EYE CAUSES YOU TO STUMBLE, GOUGE IT OUT AND THROW IT AWAY. IT IS BETTER TO LOSE ONE PART OF YOUR BODY THAN BE THROWN INTO HELL, MATTHEW 5:27!"

After this, I was just on rapid fire. I recited bible verse after bible verse to Asmodeus, and I could tell it had an effect. His two remaining heads began crying as I continued my verses, and I could hear behind his permanent smile sobs of pain. After about 5, he had fallen to the ground and began begging me to stop. He offered me anything I could ever want. He offered me lust, alcohol, women, money, anything. Even though I heard all of this, I did not stop. I continued to spill bible verses, and when he had begun to curl up into a sobbing ball, I took that as my chance.

I stabbed him in all three of his heads multiple times. He didn't even fight it, although I don't think he'd be able to anyway. As soon as I stabbed his remaining head, his body began to melt into black goop, and then the building around me began to... dissolve. It was as if it never really existed, but it was a mere illusion the entire time. Once the building started to evaporate, my mind rushed to thoughts of Millie. *"She could be in trouble!"* I thought and quickly ran to find her.

As soon as I ran out of the room and into the hallway, I found her. She looked shocked, and the demons were gone.

"Millie..?" I approached wearily.

Suddenly, she turned to face me, and she smiled. "Flynn! Dude! You'll never guess what happened! So I was like, you know, distracting these guys, and then they just slowly started to dissolve into this black goopy stuff! Totally freaky stuff!" Millie looked around and saw the building slowly vanishing. "We should get out of here and find a place to rest for the night."

I smiled and nodded my head, following Millie, finally leaving the nightclub. As soon as we stepped out of it, the entire building had disappeared, leaving no sign it was even there to begin with. The landscape turned back to normal, the dry and empty landscape of Hell. After walking for a bit,

Millie and I found a nice tree stump and laid down, finally going to bed.

Somewhere in the Core…

A minor demon quickly rushed into the room, wearing a tuxedo and carrying a letter. "Sir!"
"Oh, dear heavens! What on earth is it now?" A voice replied coldly.

The demon came closer to the man and whispered into his ear. "We've gotten word that Asmodeus has been slayed by the boy; here is a photo of his body." The demon hands the man the letter, and he examines it thoroughly and scoffs.

"Lucifer should've known Asmodeus was not fit for the job. The child is stronger than we first thought. Oh well. One must always be ready to improvise." The man sighs and

faces the demon. "Send **Belphegor** *after the child; I am curious as to how this may play out…*"

Chapter Five

I opened my eyes to see that I was in a beautiful field of flowers with bees and butterflies surrounding me. I reached out to touch the flowers, which were soft as silk. I smelt them; they smelt lovely. I continued to wonder, and there was a pond with fish, dragonflies, and even frogs. This place was beautiful. Soon, I heard a voice. The voice was loud, but it didn't scare me; in fact, it made me even calmer than before.

"Hello, my child," the voice began, "welcome to my escape. This is the only place where my fallen angel cannot take. This is my headspace."
I looked around for the voice, and ahead of me, I saw a bright light. It was just an orb of bright white light, yet I felt such a warm and calm aura from it. I immediately knew who it was.

"God?" I asked, "Is that you, my heavenly father?"

The orb moved closer to me, and the energy it was emitting was even stronger than before.

"My child, I have come to allow you to know that you will have to face your next challenge. You shall next face the prince of gluttony and the prince of envy, **Beelzebub and Leviathan**."

"But father, we just faced Asmodeus! Not to question your knowledge, but why can't we just avoid him and move straight to the Core?" I asked, anxiously fidgeting with my hands.

"My child, in order to free me and complete your quest, you must face all seven of the princes of Hell. There is no avoiding this, for this is your destiny."

I fidgeted with my hands more, my anxiety visible. I knew this was true, but I didn't want to admit that I'd have to fight all seven of the seven deadly sins. Even though I was scared, I nodded. I have to accept my destiny.

"Do not fear, for I will be with you every step of the way. I shall be watching over you and protecting you as best as I can with my limited power. You will do great things, my child. I know of it. You are stronger than you think, and whenever you doubt yourself, I will be here to give you the strength to face the challenge."

Hearing his words calmed me, and I nodded confidently. "You're right, my lord; thank you for your help. I will not let you down."

"I know you were my child. Now, go on; your quest awaits you."

And with those words, I opened my eyes, and I was back in Hell. I sat up and rubbed my eyes, looking over to where Millie was sleeping. She was already awake and was studying her hands. She looked like she had been crying.

"Millie?" I asked, "What's wrong?"

Millie whipped around quickly to face me, and she just smiled and shook her head.

"Oh. Remember how I uhm- told you that my soul had been corrupted…?"

I nervously nodded my head. "Oh no, Millie, what happened?"

She then showed me her hands. Her fingertips were turning… *black*... as if they were rotting. I heard about this back in Safe Haven. Stories of the saints venturing out, getting corrupted, and slowly turning into demons, but I never had seen it firsthand. I stared in shock as the top of her fingertips began to look rotted and began splitting. Suddenly, Millie started crying. I immediately hugged her tightly as she sobbed into my shoulder.

"I-" she barely managed to get out between sobs. "I don't know w-what to do… I don't want to be the very thing I hate. I refuse, I refuse, I refuse…" She just continued to repeat *"I refuse"* under her breath as I comforted her. Hearing her cry and seeing she was turning into the thing we were fighting against made me tear up. I was never good with emotions; I always had to be the *"stronger big brother,"* so whenever

Ness would break down in front of me, all I could do was stay silent and cry with him. Tears began streaming down my face as I hugged her, but I quickly wiped them away. Truthfully, I was just as scared as her. I'm just 14; I never asked for any of this.

Eventually, Millie's sobs calmed down, and she backed up from my hug. "Oof, ha, sorry, that kinda just uhm, slipped out." Millie joked, her face red with embarrassment and wiping away her tears. All I did was smile. I wanted to make sure she was okay, but I didn't really have the words to ask.

"Anyways!" Millie stood up, "we've wasted enough time! Let's do this thing!" Millie began to walk off, but I stopped her.

"Wait!" I grabbed her hand to stop her, "I had a dream. God visited me; he told me that we have to fight all of the seven princes of Hell…"

Millie looked at me with disbelief. "What-? Oh no. I can't do that again. Did you not notice we almost *died* back there?!

We can't do that another six times!" Millie laughed, looking at me like I was crazy.

"I know, I know, but we really don't have a choice! If we want to make it to the Core, we're going to have to go through them, and actually, we only have to fight five more."

Millie shook her head and murmured something under her breath. "God, why did I even come with you? Fine! Fine! Whatever! Let's go!" Millie started walking away again, and I ran up to her to catch up.

"Look, we can't fight each other if we want to get to the Core; we have to get along."

"Who said we were fighting?" Millie asked coldly, keeping her eyes ahead of her. "We aren't fighting; I said it's okay, now let's go, we're wasting time."

I just rolled my eyes and sighed. "Okay, whatever you say." We continued walking in silence; the tension was so thick you could cut it with a knife. After about only five minutes of walking, we began to notice a change in the atmosphere. I started to smell... *food...* food that smelt so good, and it was even worse considering I only brought bread with me. The closer the smells got, the whole scenery changed, exactly like what happened with Asmodeus. Soon, a large building with lines of people was spotted in the distance.

As we approached the building, it became clear that it was a high-end restaurant, or at least, it was trying to disguise itself as one. The closer we got, the more details were noticed. The whole building was plated with gold, it was big with multiple stories, and it had a big gold sign that read *"B&L."* But there was something terribly wrong. There were... flies... flies everywhere.

Soon, a man wearing a chef outfit emerged from the restaurant. He was a huge, fat man but had sweet eyes and such a kind smile. As soon as he left the restaurant, the people began crowding around, just like with Asmodeus, but unlike Asmodeus, he talked to them kindly and smiled. Except... every time he spoke, flies flew out of his mouth.

As soon as his eyes met ours, he smiled kindly and asked to be excused, which the people obeyed. He approached us.

"Ah! There you two are! Come in, come in! I've been waiting for you!" He said kindly, but flies spilled out of his mouth each time he talked. Alive, flying flies. He began to guide us into the restaurant. Millie and I just shared a look and awkwardly followed him into the restaurant. As soon as we entered, the smells hit immediately and were so much stronger than before. He led us both to a table and sat us down, giving us both menus.

"Here you two are! Why, hello, you too! My name is Beelzebub, and I will be taking care of you today! May I get you two something to drink?" He smiled so kindly that it was hard to say no to him.
"Uhm-" I began, fidgeting with the strap of my bag nervously, "I'll uh- I'll just have water, please."

"Perfect! And you lovely young lady?"

"Uh- well- uh-" Millie looked over at me for support, and I just gave her a slight nod. "I'll have water too…"

"That sounds incredible! I'll get that for you two right away!" His smile faded a bit as he looked at Millie, and then he took a seat at our table. "Child, I can tell something is troubling you. I can sense… *envy…*" His smile grew, and he glanced over to me. "You, dear, are jealous of *him!*" He pointed at me and chuckled. Millie turned to face me, obviously scared and uncomfortable. "Give me a second, young one, I will fetch my partner, **Leviathan…**"

He then left the both of us alone. I turned to face Millie, a small expression of fear and worry across my face. "Millie… You don't have to be envious of me! Remember, we're in this too." I was cut off by a tall man who had scaly dark skin, like a serpent, and small details that looked like horns.

"Hello you two…" He said, grinning widely. "My partner explained to me that someone here is a bit *envious* of the other, and luckily, that is just my specialty, and I can help you out…"

He then turned to Millie and gently pulled a card out of his suit. "Hear this, I will give you this card, and if you accept this, you may change your fate. You and he will switch lives, and you can stop worrying about listening to his rules and thoughts; you can just rest, and the quest will end." He then handed her a card, and on the card was my face inside a pentagram. "Think about it, dear; I will be back with your food." He then left us both alone with the card.

I looked at Millie in horror as she shakily took the card in her hands and examined it. I watched as she turned the card around, and there were instructions on the back to activate it. All she had to do was place the card in the candle on our table and wait until it all burned. With just that, she could end our quest and take over my life.

"Millie-" I barely managed to get out as my breathing got shaky and my fidgeting got worse. "Millie, please don't..."

Millie didn't respond; she just looked at the card coldly while studying it. The photo of me changed every few minutes; at first, it was a pentagram, but now it was an image of me burning as a demon. Only a few seconds later, Millie and I were taken out of our trance when we were interrupted by Beelzebub and Leviathan walking over to our table.

"Here is your food, children!" Beelzebub exclaimed, flies flying out of his mouth. He put down a plate of steak in front of me and a plate of lobster in front of Millie. Steak is my favorite food, and I didn't even order it or say anything about it. I looked in shock at the steak; it looked so… ***good…*** Millie looked at her lobster in awe, her mouth practically drooling.

"Well, come on!" The chef started happily, "Take a bite!"

I looked at Millie nervously, and she gave me a slight nod as she raised her fork.

"My soul is already corrupted… I'll be okay." She said sternly. Then, she crushed the card in her hand. Leviathan watched her crush the card, and his eyes flashed with anger, but his eerie smile remained. Millie cut into the lobster and

took a bite, but as soon as she did, both of our food turned into disgusting buzzing flies. Millie gagged, and flies flew out of her mouth. The flies all started surrounding Beelzebub and Leviathan, and they began to laugh. The flies surrounded the two of them, so we could just barely see them, but the little we could see was horrifying. Their bodies were...
Melting together...

Millie started crying and throwing up as more and more flies flew out of her mouth in place of the lobster piece she had eaten. I watched in fear as Beelzebub started growing wings like a fly, and many eyes began appearing all over his face. I looked around and saw all the other customers began to turn into many flies, and I rushed over to surround the two men.

Once all the flies left Beezelbub and Leviathan, their new form was revealed. They had two enormous wings and hundreds of eyes all around their face, and the most disturbing part was that their heads didn't seem to be able to melt all the way together; so they still had two heads, but they looked like they had been burned and melted together by a fire. I grabbed my dagger out of my bag and jumped over the table, running.

"MILLIE!" I shouted, "RUN!"

That's all I had to say to get Millie to run with me. We ran, even though we had no idea where we were running to. The restaurant was so large that it seemed like there was no possible exit. As we ran, I heard the buzzing of flies close behind me. I swung behind me mindlessly with my dagger, but I barely did any damage. I may have gotten ten flies at most. Yeah, not much.

"FLYNN!" Millie yelled at me, and I quickly faced her, still running. "GIVE ME YOUR PIECE OF BREAD!" I didn't even question her; I just threw her the piece of bread I had left. As soon as she caught it, she immediately threw it to her right, and right away, all the flies and the monstrosity that was once Beelzebub and Leviathan flew over to the bread, fighting over it. It looked like the two men still had minds of their own, and they were fighting violently over the piece of bread. I saw my opportunity and swung my dagger at full force at them. They screamed out in anguish as I managed to cut their wings badly, but as soon as I did this, they used their arms to hit me away.

I flew back and hit my head violently against the floor, and my dagger fell from my hands. The last thing I remembered before blacking out was Millie grabbing my dagger and rushing at Beelzebub and Leviathan. After that, all I saw ***was black…***

Eventually, though, I did wake up. I woke up to Millie sitting on the ground with me, holding my head up and whispering to me to please get up. I tried to sit up, but a sharp pain in my head stopped me. I looked up at Millie, who was now smiling and had tears streaming down her face.

"T-there you are!" She said softly, wiping her tears away. I saw blood on her hands, and it clicked. I touched my head and saw my hand covered in blood. I started freaking out.

"Hey, hey! It's going to be okay, okay? I, uhm- I prayed and tried a Latin healing spell, and now your head looks a lot better! You'll probably still need to rest, though." Millie smiled at me warmly. I looked around and noticed black goop all over the floor, just like when I had defeated Asmodeus, and the building was fading away, too, just like last time. I smiled.

"Huh, you really did a number on that old fool, didn't you?" I joked and laughed softly.

Millie laughed and wiped away her tears. "Yeah, I uh- guess you could say that." She smiled and looked away. "Why don't we rest here tonight? I don't really think you're fit for traveling. He really got you."

I smiled and closed my eyes. "Yeah, you're right. Let's just rest for the rest of the day; we have time."

Then, we did just that. We rested, hopeful, and ready for our next challenge.

Somewhere in the Core...

The two men watched as Flynn and Millie rested in Beelzebub's once large and beautiful restaurant.

"Huh… So the children were able to take down Beelzebub just like that; this may be a problem."
"Lucifer, he is only the second strongest prince. We'll be okay. Besides, the girl has already been corrupted; she has limited time yet. And as it seems, he cannot take down the princes without her assistance."

One of the voices, supposedly Lucifer, nodded and turned off the TV screen where they were watching Flynn and Mille. "We will send **Mammon** after them. The boy is injured, so it'll be easier to either kill him and let him burn in Hell with the other saints or finally corrupt him and put an end to his quest. Damian, go fetch Mammon now."

The other mysterious voice, now known as Damian, answered sharply and coldly. "I will not **fetch** your little henchman for you, Lucifer. I have far more important things to do. I thought we already established this."

Lucifer's eyes flashed a deep red, and he pinned Damian up against the wall. **"You forget who you speak to, Damian. No one talks to me like that."**

Damian's eyes turned black, and suddenly, Lucifer was flung across the room away from him. Damian watched coldly as Lucifer struggled on the ground, and he fixed his collar.

"And you forget who gave you all this power. I could bring you to your knees whenever I please. So, as I was saying, go have someone else get Mammon because I have important things that need to be done."

Suddenly, a door opened, and Lilith walked in. She stared awkwardly at the two men before speaking. "I have recovered enough to fight; I can fight them again. I won't let you down this time.

Damian just rolls his eyes, "Get the hell out of here, you worthless slut, you had your chance, and you failed. I don't even know why we keep you around. You're only here because you're Lucifer's little play toy." Damian scoffed and grabbed her violently by her arm, throwing her onto the ground along with Lucifer. "Plus, you forget where you stand next to me, woman. I tell you where you can go and when you can speak." Damian looked at Lilith, awaiting a response. She gave him a cold look, and his eyes flashed black.

Lilith looked at Damian with fear in her eyes, and she quickly nodded. "Y-yes, sir… I… I won't interrupt you again…"

Damian smiled sinisterly and nodded. "That's what I want to hear from a whore like you. Now, I am going to get more cameras on the children so I can watch them closer."

With that, Damian turned away from Lucifer and Lilith, who were still on the ground and left the room, slamming the door behind him.

Chapter Six

I opened my eyes and realized I was in the same garden. The sun was on my skin, and I was lying on a yellow flower bed. I sat up and saw the same bright, warm light that I had known as God.

"Welcome back, my child." The light said gently, "You have made me proud. Your friend, Millie, has done well. She took good care of you, Flynn."
I smiled and nodded, "Yeah, she's a good friend." I blush, embarrassed. "You have called me back here for something, correct? I'm assuming I have another challenge." I say, nervously fiddling with my hands.

The orb of light grew brighter and became warmer, calming my nerves. "Yes, my child, you will have to face the prince of greed, **Mammon**."

"But! Father, my head! I have gotten badly hurt; how can I face another challenge so quickly?"

"Feel your head, my child."

I slowly reached up to feel my head, and I realized it was healed. It wasn't perfect, I would definitely have a concussion, but I was healed enough to keep going.

I smile and face the orb, and I get on my knees in a prayer position. "Thank you so much, my lord! Thank you so much for everything you've done for me on my quest. I truly appreciate it, and I will free you and the other saints; I will make you proud."
The orb approached me, and the light surrounded me, almost as if giving me a hug. The light was so calming, and it just gave me even more courage to go on. I felt as if nothing could stop me now.

"One last thing before you go, my child. You will not be able to face the following few challenges with just you and Millie. Due to this, I shall send one of my best angels, Michael, to help you. He will make the subsequent battles easy, but once you face… **Damian…** you will have to face him alone. Due to the help of… **his black magic,** he has become more vital than ever before. Therefore, I can only protect you up until then. Even after all that is said, I still have hope in you, my child. You can and **will** do this; I believe in you.

"Wait!" I yelled, "Who is Damian?!"

He did not answer; everything just got darker until I opened my eyes, and I was back in Hell. I felt my head and realized it was just how God had said; it was healed. Of course, it still hurts a bit, but I would be okay. Besides, now I would have the strength of God's most significant angel, Michael, on my side. I looked around and noticed Millie and I were still in the same position as her, holding my head in her hands. She was asleep. I sat up and saw that the black goop was still there from Millie killing Beelzebub.

I gently nudged Millie to wake her up, and she stretched and yawned. "Hey dude-" she said sleepily. We must've stayed there for hours.

"I had another dream; we have to fight Mammon next."

Millie looked at me with fear, her face going pale momentarily before she shook it off. "But what about your head?"

I turned around to let her see the back of my head. It was healed.

"Holy crap, dude... Did your dream do that?"

I nodded and sighed. "Yeah, it still kinda hurts, but I'll be fine." I look around nervously and fidget with my shirt. "Oh, in my dream, I was also told that we'll start to get help now. God told me he'd send *Michael* to help us defeat everyone, including facing... Lucifer..."

Millie put her head in her hands and cursed under her breath. Eventually, she looked back up at me with a face full of annoyance and dread. "We have to face Lucifer?"

I nodded slowly, and she sighed. "Okay, well, if we're gonna have Michael with us, where is he?" I shrugged, but as soon as I did, there was a bright, blinding light. Millie and I both looked towards it and then we saw the figure of a man with wings. It was Micheal.

I stared in awe as the light got brighter and brighter, but then the light just suddenly vanished, and Michael was in front of us... Let's just say he was *not* how I remembered him. When I met him the first time, he wore beautiful armor and had beautiful flowy blonde hair. Now, well, he wore sweatpants and a hoodie, and his once flowy and majestic blonde hair was flat and greasy. Even after all of that, he still remained handsome.

"Sup," Micheal said nonchalantly as if he wasn't God's top angel. He sighed and walked closer to Millie and me, who were just staring in shock. The closer he got, the more delicate details I noticed. He had deep eyebags and many scars on his face. There were so many scars just on his face; I was scared of how many scars his hoodie and sweatpants hid.

Millie bowed down at his feet and began talking very nervously. "Oh my God! I mean, oh my gosh! It's you! H-hello, uh- our savior!"

Michael visibly cringed and took a step back, placing his hands in the pockets of his hoodie. "Uh- please don't do that. That's weird as Hell." Micheal said awkwardly, and Millie quickly stood up. "Look, guys, I'm just here because I wanna free my boss, and I wanna shove it in Lucifer's face that we won again." Micheal rolled his eyes, and he looked irritable. "Last time I saw that prick, we were arguing, and I was all like, 'well at least I wasn't cast out from Heaven and into Hell!' and he got all pissy, and he was like, 'imma put you in Hell hoe,' and I just laughed, but then he did. So now I'm pissed, and I wanna get back at him. We were originally just arguing about the body of Moses, but he wanted to be an a-hole and insult my existence! He's such a jackass."

As Michael continued to ramble on about how annoyed he was at Lucifer, Millie and I just exchanged looks. I guess being tortured in Hell really does something to your personality. In the beginning, when Micheal saved all the surviving saints, he was so kind and professional. Now, he acted like a sassy teenager.

"Anyways, what are you hoes up to?" He asked sassily, almost as if mocking us.

"Well… uhh…" I started awkwardly, "We were gonna keep making our way to the Core and, like, fight Mammon."

Michael shrugged. "Sounds good to me. So let's go y'all." He just started walking West. The Core is East.

"Uhm Micheal- the Core is the other way, it's East."

"Oh." He turned around and began walking the other way. "Well, what are you two losers waiting for? Let's go."
Millie and I quickly got up and began walking with Michael.
"Sooooo…" Millie said, "How is life?"

Michael rolled his eyes and shrugged. "I mean, I'm alive. Hell sucks, though, you know, the whole forever tortured thing. There's been a lot of drama between the angels and stuff because, like, we don't wanna be the first one tortured for the day, so we always argue who goes first." Michael looked over at Millie and smirked smugly. "After they tried to make me go first, I just pulled the 'well, I'm God's best angel, and I'll literally kill you,' and now they don't ever ask me! Wow… I'm a dick."

Millie just awkwardly laughed, as did I. Michael was a bit of a loose screw, I guess. We continued to walk in silence for a few minutes before Micheal broke it again.

"Jeez, you guys are boring! Why don't we play a game until we get there? I'll ask you guys questions, and you answer truthfully! Seems fun, right!"

Millie crossed her arms and sighed. "That doesn't sound like a game; that just sounds like you snooping."
Michael smiled, "Well, it is, but it's fun! For me, at least. Plus. *I already know everything about you. I just wanna see if you'll answer honestly.*"

"Wait, what?" I stopped walking and faced Michael. "What do you mean you know everything about us?!"

Michael smiled widely and chuckled. "I'm the only angel who can sneak out of Hell; who else do you think is your guardian angel? I watch after all of you, and I know *all* of your little secrets."

At this point, I had begun to panic a little. Of course, I was good enough to be considered a saint, but I sure as hell had my own secrets. I'm not always happy, and I hope he doesn't know about what happens when I get really low. I just continued to walk in silence, and it seemed Millie had her fair trade of secrets, too, because she did the same thing.

Michael seemed to notice this, and he sighed. He gives Millie and me a look that genuinely makes me believe he cares and shows some sympathy for at least a minute. This, although, was quickly broken by Michael's once again taunting attitude. "Awe, guys, don't cry now. You'll be fine." He raises his eyebrows and chuckles. We just walk in silence the rest of the way.

We continued to walk until, yet again, the atmosphere and surroundings began to change. All three of us looked around to see that we were now in a neighborhood, all smaller houses. Even though there were many houses, there were no people. We kept walking, and then we saw it. There was a massive mansion with fountains and pools and expensive exotic sports cars.

Michael smiled as he saw the house. "Welcome to Mammon's house, everyone!" Before we could say anything, Michael flapped his wings, flew to the entrance of the house, and knocked loudly on the door. "MAMMON! I KNOW YOUR ASS IS IN THERE OPEN UP!" Michael yelled and continued to bang on the door. As he was doing this, Millie and I also walked up to the front door.

Eventually, the door swung open, and a man was wearing a fancy tuxedo and had jewelry with diamonds all on. As soon as he saw Michael, he smiled widely, showing his teeth were replaced with diamonds. The closer we got to the house, the more we saw. The inside was decked out entirely in diamonds and gold.

"Ahhh…" Said Mammon, smiling. "What a lovely surprise. What are you doing here, Michael? I see you brought the two troublemakers over whom Lucifer and Damian are throwing a fit. I am Mammon." He looked directly at Millie and me, smiling and reaching his hand out to shake ours, but all I could think about was how he said Lucifer and… Damian? They were throwing a fit over us. Were they watching us? I began fidgeting nervously with the strap of my bag.

Michael smiled and shrugged. "Yeah, that's em'. I'm guessing you know why we're here then. We're here to beat your ass."

Mammon raised an eyebrow and smiled. "Oh, I know. I won't let that happen. I'm a lover, not a fighter." He said jokingly. "Well, since you all are here, come on in. We can talk together *civilly*." He then held the door open, smiling widely to let us in.

"Yessir!" Michael exclaimed happily, fist-bumping Mammon on the way in. Millie and I reluctantly followed inside, staying close to Michael but quickly realizing how comfortable he felt in Mammon's house. It was apparent he had been here before. He led us both to the living room, and I noticed Mammon observing us quietly as if thinking we might try to steal something. His house was decorated with lovely paintings and vases against the walls on fancy luxurious shelves.

"Here we are!" Mammon exclaimed. It was a beautiful living room with windows overlooking a huge pool and a large garden. Michael lay on the couch while Millie and I awkwardly sat on a chair.

"So…" Millie began awkwardly, "uhm- how do you know each other?"

Micheal and Mammon shared a look before they both started laughing. Michael spoke first. "Okay, okay, so basically what happened is I escaped from Hell, but like, I figured out I couldn't free the saints, so I looked around, and I met the seven princes of Hell. I hate them. I mean, they put me and my boss in literal Hell, but they're my only option to hang out with. I refuse to hang out with y'all at the Safe Haven; y'all are boring."

Both Michael and Mammon laughed, and Mammon clapped. "This is true! Oh, he always says he hates us, but I know you love us!" Mammon joked with Michael. "Ah, yes, I know why you two are here; you are here to kill me, correct? Well, let me just tell you, this guy over here has been trying for a while, and I just dodge all his attacks, so you two don't have a chance."

Millie looked offended by this and stood up, reaching into my bag, grabbing my dagger, and holding out to Mammon's neck. He just smiled, and Michael smiled, looking surprised.

"God! Shut the hell up! Stop acting so damn cocky! If you really think you're so invincible, then stand up like a man and fight me, dammit!" Millie shouted in Mammon's face; I just watched the interaction, knowing that if I got involved, I might be the one getting stabbed.

Mammon laughed mockingly and smiled teasingly. "I'm not gonna hit a little girl; you're too weak and worthless for me to even waste my energy on you." Mammon smiled sinisterly.

"GOD SHUT UP!" Millie yelled, swinging the dagger at full force at his head. Mammon smiled, and his eyes widened, and he dodged, and my dagger went straight into his couch.

I swear, for a second, when the blade hit the couch, he winced in pain, but it was only for a second before he regained himself. Millie kept swinging at him, but he kept dodging her attacks. I looked over at Michael, who seemed to be amused at this. Eventually, Millie began to slow down and stopped swinging. Mammon smiled at her mockingly.

"Finally down, sweetheart?" He said, raising an eyebrow.

Millie just clenched my dagger in her hands and gritted her teeth, looking at him with anger. She spoke angrily between her teeth, "I *know* there is a way for me to kill you, and I will find it jackass." With that, Millie stormed out of the room, and Michael and Mammon began laughing. I quickly followed behind her.

"Millie! Wait! We'll find a way to beat him!" I half yelled, running after her.

Millie turned around, and her face was just filled with anger. "FLYNN! How the *hell* do you expect us even to land a blow on him?! He dodges everything! There is no way we can take him down!"

"I think there is," I said quietly so no one but Millie could hear. "When you attacked him and hit the couch, he winced in pain! And when we were walking him, he kept watching us; I think it was to make sure we didn't damage anything! I think if we break enough of his stuff, we'll be able to weaken him enough to take him out!"

Millie sighed and smiled. "Jeez, Flynn, you are way too observant for your own good. I think you have a point, though; we can at least try." Millie looked around and saw a nearby vase. "Let's test your theory." Before I could object, she threw the vase hard against the floor, making it shatter into hundreds of pieces. As soon as she did this, we heard a scream coming from the living room we just came from. It was Mammon. He was screaming and cussing in pain; it seems like I said right.

Millie looked at me and smiled, and I nodded. That was our confirmation. We began to run around the halls, smashing and breaking anything in our paths like reckless toddlers.

"W-WHERE THE HELL ARE THOSE LITTLE SHITS?!" Yelled Mammon. It was now clear he was looking for us, and he was obviously taking damage. Suddenly, off in the distance, I heard another smash that Millie or I did not do. We listened to a familiar voice yell out to Mammon.

"TAKE THAT YOU ASSHOLE! THAT'S FOR PUTTING ME IN HELL!" It was Michael.

Mammon screamed out in pain, and there was a loud crash behind us. Millie and I looked back and saw Mammon crawling on the ground to us. His legs were broken. That's why he was screaming in pain; every time we broke one of his objects, it broke one of his bones. I stared in horror as I saw his bones tearing out of his skin and him dragging around in a pool of blood. This was our chance, our time. I grabbed my dagger from Millie and ran at full force, plunging my dagger into his head with all my strength and stabbing him multiple times.

I don't even remember how many times I stabbed him; I just know I kept stabbing. Mammon screamed in pain as his blood flew up and stained my clothes and my face. I just kept going.

Eventually, I stopped. I looked up and saw Michael looking down at me, smiling. "Damn, kid, didn't know you had that in you." I looked down and saw his body slowly turning into black goop, and the mansion was slowly fading away. I looked back at Millie, who was looking at me proudly but also looked shocked.

"Can we… can we just leave?" I asked quietly, and Michael smiled and nodded. He didn't even let me register anything before he grabbed me, picked me up, and threw me over his shoulder like a bag. "Wait- What- Let me down!" I tried to get down, but Michael was far stronger than me. I guess he is God's archangel for a reason.

Millie grabbed my bag and put my dagger in it, following closely behind us as we began making our way to the next challenge, which Michael said would be the prince of sloth, **Belphegor.**

Somewhere in the Core...

"Hmmm... they seemed to have easily defeated Mammon, seeing right through his scheme immediately," Damian said to himself, watching the screen of me, Millie, and Michael closely. Suddenly, the door slammed open, and Lucifer entered the room.

"THEY HAVE DEFEATED MAMMON! IT IS ONLY A MATTER OF TIME UNTIL THEY MAKE IT THROUGH BELPHEGOR AND SATAN AND THEN ME! I cannot allow

them to take me down so easily! I cannot wait to see the look on their faces when I destroy them... They do not stand a chance against me and my superior power! I am sure to be victorious, and I will revel in their demise! With my brilliant plan, there is no way-" Lucifer stops and looks to the screen showing all three of us. *"...is that fucking Michael...?!"*

Chapter Seven

I jolted upwards as the hard ground and rocks were thrown against my body. "HEY!" I looked up at Michael, who was looking at me coldly and had just dropped me on the ground. "Dude… Why??" Michael didn't say anything; he just walked off, and I forced myself off the ground as Millie gave him a sour look. I watched in confusion as Michael gathered sticks and dirt, laying them on the ground as if he were to start a fire.

"Hey…" I began speaking, dazed from the fall. "What are you doing?"

Michael didn't look back at me; he gathered dirt and sticks. "Making dinner."

Millie and I shared confused looks. "What?" Millie spoke up. Michael rolled his eyes and finally turned back to look at us.

"I'm making dinner, like, food? You know you can cook here, right? How else do you think we eat?" Michael then turned back around and murmured something under his breath.

"I honestly thought you didn't." Millie says, crossing her arms.

I looked at Michael, amazed, as he rubbed the sticks together, making a spark appear. Soon enough, the wood had caught on fire. We watched, intrigued, as he grabbed the handful of dirt and put his hands above the fire. The dirt began to bubble.

"What the... That- that isn't supposed to happen-" I said, chuckling a bit in shock.

Michael looked back at us smugly and smirked. "Bon appetit, baby." He then raised the boiling dirt to his mouth and began to eat it. His face scrunched up in disgust, but he swallowed it anyway. "It isn't the best tasting, but it's filling and will keep you from starving out here."

He sits back, grabs more dirt, and repeats the process a few times, his face looking as though he may vomit at any moment. He holds out some of the dirt, offering it to me, and instinctively, Millie and I shake our heads. Michael scoffs and continues to eat reluctantly. "I wasn't offering you any." I look at Micheal, confused, but he shakes his head and points to Millie. "I was talking to her. I don't like her; she can find her own food."

"You know, you don't always have to be such a dick." Millie said, furrowing her eyebrows and crossing her arms.

"Don't talk to me like that. I'm your damn savior, your only way to get out of here." Michael replied with a smirk, taking another mouthful of the dirt.

"We were doing just fine without you. You can't even fight the sins; we were the ones who defeated them!" Millie replied, her voice rising. Michael seemed to get under her skin pretty quickly.

Micheal's face grew into a slight scowl, staring daggers at Millie, Flynn just in the middle. "You know," Millie began again, "You used to be tolerable when you took me to the Safe Haven and everything."

"What?-" I said. I didn't know anything happened between Millie and Michael. As I tried to question the two about it, Michael stood up and began to yell at Millie, interrupting me.

"You are a bitch, you know that! You think after all these damn years in fucking captivity, you wouldn't change!? Knowing you can't help your creator, the person who helped and loved you without expecting anything in return? I don't want to hear your bullshit, Millie."

Millie was quick to stand up and yell back at the enraged angel. "Did you forget that happened to Flynn and me? How long have we been stuck in that stupid Safe Haven? You don't see me coming up with half-assed excuses on why I can be a shitty person!" Millie sighed and stared at Michael with rage before turning away. "I can't do this. I'm out." Millie then turned and walked off, not saying anything else, disappearing off into the distance.

Michael sighed, murmuring something in annoyance, taking another scoopful of the dirt. The tension in the air could be cut with a knife, and I didn't handle silence well; I needed to speak up.

"So, uhm, what was that about? Did you guys know each other beforehand or something?" I asked, fidgeting with the straps of my bag.

"No, we met at the same time I met everyone else." Michael replied coldly, the silence filling the air and creeping into my ears like bugs.

"Should we go after her?" I asked again, trying to make some kind of conversation.

"No, she'll be back soon." Michael said, this time relaxing and looking over to me, who was still anxiously fiddling with the strap of my bag. Michael saw how I nervously messed with my bag, and his expression softened. "Hey, you okay? Of course, you aren't. You're what? 14? 15? And you're trying to be killed by the literal devil." Michael sighed, and I looked over to him. "You know, it must seem pretty good for me. I'm the only angel who can leave the hell Lucifer trapped us in. I'm supposed to be the super strong, wise angel, but I was scared shitless when Hell started to fight us and won. God sent me to take all the survivors, and He knows that I was hunted along the way. Then I figured out I could leave Hell, so I tried to fight the seven deadly sins, but each time, I failed, and they laughed in my face. What else could I do after that but accept my fate? I tried to befriend them, and it worked. They just befriended me because they knew that with that damn black magic machine, I couldn't hurt them, and they couldn't kill me; no one can kill an angel. We're immortal."

Michael sighed and looked over to me, who was listening intently. "Sorry about rambling on to you about this; you're a kid; you shouldn't even hear about this."

"No, it's okay. I understand how you feel." I said with a smile, looking at the ground. "When Hell broke loose, I was nine and terrified. My mom hid me and my brother in a box and taped us up. I thought we were going to die. Honestly, even now, I wish I would've died in that box. I consider it a lot, you know, like, killing myself. I think anything would be better than being stuck in the Safe Haven. The only reason why I'm still alive is Ness, my brother. I couldn't leave him, I couldn't break him like that, plus, isn't it like a sin? I tried once, maybe like a year ago. I tried to stab myself with my dagger, but I couldn't bring myself to. Ness was supposed to be at school, but he came home early and walked in when I was supposed to do it. He didn't realize what I was doing, but it was a wake-up call for me. It snapped me out of it, and I just focused on working and providing for Ness. Sometimes, I still feel like that, but it isn't as bad as before."

Michael listened intently and nodded, sighing, a look of sadness across his face. The two of us stayed silent after that, just thinking about our pasts and stories. Michael, however, eventually spoke up.

"I'll take up your advice; we should look for Millie. It's been a minute since we've seen her again."

I nodded and stood up, clutching my bag. "Yeah, let's go find her."

Chapter Eight

The two of us continued to walk toward where Millie was, and we could sense the danger that came. The more we walked, the more we noticed the scenery changing. She had gotten caught by one of the deadly sins. We saw how the environment turned to one of a calming beach, and we soon noticed Millie, who was lying down in a hammock, her eyes closed.

Immediately when I saw her, I rushed over and tried to shake her awake. I felt as if my heart stopped, realizing she wasn't responding to my shakes, and I backed up.

She's dead. I thought.

Or, at least for five seconds before I felt a hand on my shoulder. I swiftly whipped my head around, only to be met with… An old man?

"Don't worry, son, she ain't dead. She's just taking a nap!" The older man said with a smile. He didn't look like any of the other seven deadly sins we faced; he just looked like a random lazy- oh. Lazy.

"Are you… Belphegor…? The sin of sloth?" I asked nervously, glancing over at Millie, standing beside her as if trying to protect her resting body.

The old man smiled, and out of nowhere, a woman came up behind him in a suit, handing him a glass of alcohol as he sat down on a lounge chair next to Millie.

"I prefer the term 'lazy'. Sloth is just a weird word to say." The old man, now known as Belphegor, said with a smirk as he closed his eyes, crossing his arms behind his head to make himself more comfortable. "I know you two three have had such a hard journey! Why not relax a little?"

Michael and I shared a look before Michael spoke up for me. "Yeah, no. We'll be leaving now. Give us back the girl, " Michael said sternly and sharply, getting closer to Belphegor and trying to intimidate him. Belphegor just smiled and replied.

"No, can do. Your little 'friend' here has already given in to me." He said with a smile, his eyes narrowing.

"She what," Michael said, his eyebrows furrowing with anger and confusion. I watched the whole ordeal from the side, still softly shaking Millie to wake her.

"Oh? She didn't tell you? Well, she told the other gentlemen here, I can tell by how he reacted."

Michael looked back at me, shaking his head dismissively. "She- what? How didn't I know- I'm supposed to know everything about these brats-" Michael turned back to Belphegor, his face full of anger.

"Wait, I see you're mad. Maybe we've gotten off on the wrong foot." Belphegor said with a smile, raising his hands defensively. "Here, let's start over, what's your guy's name?"

Michael suddenly looked very offended. "Did you seriously just ask me my name?"

Belphegor needed clarification. "I'm sorry, but that's the polite thing to do when meeting someone new!" He said with a confused smile.

Michael let out a sharp scoff and looked around the area. "There's no way you're not messing with me right now. I'm Michael?"

"Doesn't ring a bell!" Belphegor hummed.

"We fight all the time!" Michael said in annoyance.

"Ah! You're the one who tore my shirt! I remember you now!"

"What- no! I didn't tear your- you seriously don't remember me!?"

"I see a lot of new faces! You can't expect me to remember everyone I come in contact with. That's just way too much effort!"

Michael scoffed, annoyed at the disinterest and disregard for him. Finally, I spoke up.

"Sorry, sir. We're going to chat in private real quick. We'll be back!" I said, ushering Michael, who was still glaring at Belphegor. After we were at a safe distance from the old man, I began to chat with Michael.

"Michael, why haven't you tried to kill!" I asked, in a whisper shout.

"Did you seriously already forget my backstory event? I can't! When that dumbass decided to make Lucifer that- that machine- all the seven sins grew more powerful than ever. I can't defeat them, and if I try to fight him, he'll just get mad and try to hurt you, and I can't have that."

"Oh," I said as I pondered our earlier fight with Beelzebub. "Then why were you able to fight Beelzebub?"

"That's because you had already weakened him."

"Why hadn't you tried doing that before?"

Michael sighed and looked away. "You do ask a lot of questions, huh?" Michael looked back at me, who was just waiting for his answer. He sighed and continued. "I gave up trying to figure out what I could do to take over the sins and break that machine to free the saints, but after many failed attempts, I just gave up."

I just nodded and stood there momentarily, thinking about what to do. I could only think of trying to grab Millie and go. Since Belphegor was the sin of sloth, maybe he'd be too lazy to fight us and just let us go.

"Okay," I began, ready to tell Michael my plan. "So he's the sin of sloth, right? So maybe he'll be too lazy to fight us and just let us go!"

"Honestly," Michael replied with a long sigh, "that's one of the stupidest ideas I've ever heard, but I don't have a better one, so let's do it." He said with a shrug.

I smiled and nodded, happy that he quickly agreed to my plan. We walked back over to where Belphegor was lying down next to Millie. Michael and I gave an awkward nod before scooping her up into our arms and beginning to leave. We were stopped by a servant of Belphegor, who stood in our way, a stoic expression on her face.

"Ah ah ah," Belphegor said with a chuckle. "You think it's *that* easy? Servants, take care of them." Belphegor then laughed and just sipped on his martini.

Dozens of servants soon surrounded Michael and me as they pulled swords from pockets we had not noticed before.

"What-" Michael began but was soon interrupted by one of the servants charging at him, slicing his cheek open, allowing his golden blood to flow. For a moment, I just stared at him, stunned.

I didn't know angels could get hurt.

Michael's eyes darkened with anger. "So, that's how they want to play?" He muttered, licking the golden blood that trickled down his cheek.

"Guess we have to give them a game they'll never forget," I replied, my heart pounding as I grabbed my dagger in one swift movement.

We sprung into action, my blade swiftly finding its place in one of the nearby servant's chests. The servant let out a hiss before Michael grabbed its sword, leaving it as it crumbled to dust. Michael, with his newfound sword, was a whirlwind beside me. His sword shone in the light, striking the servants with divine precision, which only an angel could pull off. The two of us were an unstoppable duo, dancing to the song of justice. The servants fought back with mindless rage but were no match for the two of us.

Michael thrust his swords from one servant to the next, then spun around, the blade catching another demon's neck, sending her hissing while crumbling to the ground, just a pile of dust. The two of us were good, but the stampede of demons kept coming, relentless and unforgiving.

Belphegor watched with a mocking smile, swirling his drink with his fingertip. "Is that all you got?" he taunted, his voice calm and low. He leaned back in his chair, looking too relaxed, as if he didn't have a care in the world.

Michael's eyes flickered to mine, his face and hands covered in golden angel blood, and that's when I noticed I was too covered in cuts. I was too busy fighting to see before. "Distract him," I whispered. Michael nodded, his wings snapping out in a blinding flare of light. His wings were gorgeous, and I, too, had to shelter my eyes not to be blinded.

The last time I saw his wings, they weren't blinding. It was something he could control.

Belphegor raised an arm to shield, just for an instant, but it was enough. I rushed forward, ducking beneath the swing of a servant's blade, and I was on him. Belphegor's eyes widened in surprise, his grin fading into something else- anger, maybe even fear.

I drove my sword upward, aiming for his throat. But he was quick, too quick, and could knock my blade from my hand with a simple backhand. "Nice try," he sneered, his voice low and hot on my face. I could smell the alcohol on him and could feel the heat of his body radiating off me like a furnace.

Michael seized the opportunity, leaping into the air with a mighty flap of his wings. He brought the sword down in a brilliant arc, and like thunder, Belphegor's head was severed clean off from his shoulder. The demon's body twitched, and it felt as if he was still alive for a moment. Then it collapsed, lifeless, as the head rolled away into the dust.

There was a moment of silence, and then a wail erupted from the servants, a sound of pure despair. Without their master, they were lost and confused. One by one, they began to crumble, turning to ash and blowing away in the wind.

I dropped to my knees beside Millie as Michael watched from the side, attempting to catch his breath. My hands shook as I reached out to touch her skin, which had become pale, too pale, and her breath swallowed. For a moment, I thought she wouldn't wake up. Then her eyes fluttered open, and she looked up at me with a faint smile. "Took you long enough,' she murmured, weak but alive. I looked down at her hands; they were now entirely black and rotten. It seemed that since we were in the place where her soul had been corrupted, it sped up the process of her turning into a sinner.

"Yeah, sorry," I replied, grinning despite the situation. "Had to take out the trash first." I then looked over to Michael, seeing all his cuts, his face and hands covered in golden blood. "Are you okay, Michael?" I asked, my voice laced with concern.

He gave a small, tired smile. "I'll be fine," he replied. "Angels can't die. Let's leave here before the place goes down and rest."

Millie and I nodded, and the three of us made our way out of the crumbling area. We only had two more of the seven deadly sins to go.

Somewhere in The Core...

Lucifer peered through the doorway. It had been days since Damian left his room to watch the three plow through the deadly sins.

"Damian." Lucifer began, "They now have Michael on their side. I have already told my brother, Satan, to face them and destroy them."

"Good," Damian replied, his eyes not leaving the screen that watched Flynn and the others.

Lucifer sighed and furrowed his brows. "Damian, I am worried for you. You haven't left the room in days, and I need you to remember your end of the bargain."

Immediately, Damian's eyes darkened, and he turned his chair to face the devil. "Excuse me?" He said with a smirk as he stood up from his chair and began to walk towards Lucifer. "Have you forgotten who made the machine? Who gives you your power?"

As soon as Damian said this, Lucifer was quick to snap back. "And have **you** forgotten who gives you the power to run it? Or who gives you power at all? Don't forget that we need each other, and if they can kill me, you will be nothing but fish for a shark."

As Lucifer said this, he turned back around and left the room, and Damian just sighed and sat back down at the chair, obsessing over the saviors, waiting eagerly for their next fight.

Chapter Nine

I groaned as we continued to walk, and Michael and I tried to hold Millie up for support. Michael looked annoyed that he had to help her but said nothing, regardless. I brought my hand up to feel my face, which was still leaking blood from our recent fight. I looked over at Michael, his face also bleeding. After walking for a while, we just decided to stop and rest.

Michael and I softly put Millie onto the ground, who was regaining her strength. "Okay," Micheal began, "we should rest here for a minute. Wait, how many of the seven sins have you fought so far?" Michael questioned.
I thought for a minute, fiddling with the strap of my well; that was the 5th deadly sin so far. We only have two to go."

"You only have- shit." Michael groaned, frustrated. "You haven't fought Lucifer or Satan yet? Have you?"

I felt my face go pale, and I saw that Millie did, too. We had to face the last two most substantial sins: wrath and pride.

"He won't let us rest, especially now since Millie is weakened. He's going to fight us."

When Michael said this, the sky above us darkened and turned blood red. The ground trembled below us, a deep rumble that seemed to come from the Earth's very core. Michael gripped the sword he had stolen from Belphegor's servants, Millie getting up and glancing around the terrain nervously. I grabbed my dagger, tightening my grip around it, and I swear that just for a moment, it glowed. It glowed with divine light, and I knew *I was the chosen one.*

My knuckles grew white from my firm grip on my dagger, my heart pounding in my ears. This was all too soon; we had just faced Belphegor. How would we pull this off? Could I genuinely stand against Satan? The prince of Wrath, with only a dagger and the power of God on my side? I heard a voice calling me, and I immediately knew who it was. It wasn't God, it was Ness. He said one simple sentence.

I believe in you.

I suddenly felt that we could do this. I had more hope. Michael stood tall beside me, his wings stretched wide and shimmering in the red light. His expression was fierce and stoic, his blue eyes narrowing in concentration, shifting his eyes swiftly along the empty land. "Stay close," he murmured. His voice was low but firm. "This will get a lot worse before it gets better."

Millie was on the other side of me, standing close to me as her hands moved delicately as she began to weave an intricate spell. Her face was set in determination, her brows furrowed as she whispered a spell in Latin, one she had earlier been trying to teach me. Small balls of sweat trickled down her forehead as she charged the spell.

"Flynn," she said, her voice steady despite the tension, "this is it. Remember, you're stronger than you think. We've faced demons before. Remember why you're here."

I nodded, swallowing hard, my blessed dagger feeling oddly heavy yet light all at once in my hand. "Got it," I replied, my voice sounding far more uncertain and shaky than intended.

Then, without warning, Satan lunged.

His movements were impossibly fast, a blur of darkness and fire. He wielded a massive sword that he had arched down to fall directly onto us with speed that defied all logic. I could barely dodge it, and when the sword hit the ground, the impact was so hard it almost threw me to my knees. The heat was unbearable; the very air around us seemed to have caught on fire.

Michael was there in an instant, his wings propelling him forward, his sword meeting with Satan's with a clash of metal that rang out like the city bells that we once had.

"Focus!" Michael yelled to me, snapping me out of the trance that the impact of Satan's sword had put me into. "Keep your mind clear, Flynn!"

I steadied myself, feeling the determination and fear once again pulse through my veins, but this wasn't the time to have fear or doubt; this was the reason I was put in this Hell. I rushed to Satan with my dagger, the blade connecting with his side, and there was a flash of light. A burst of divine energy seemed to burn him, even if only for a little, but I could see a drop of black dripping from his side where the blade had come into contact with his skin. Satan roared, though not a roar of pain but of rage, but it was enough for us.

Satan's body twisted around, his neck stretching out, and the beautiful body he had presented himself with, as did all the other princes, began to distort himself. His eyes locked onto mine, filled with fury. "You are the Chosen One," he hissed, his voice like nails on a chalkboard. "You wield power you do not understand. I will rip your soul apart and feast on your agony."

I didn't flinch, attempting not to show any signs of fear, yet on the inside, I was shaking. "Not today," I muttered, more to myself than anyone else.

Across the field, I heard Millie's voice grow louder, her spell reaching a fever pitch. I could feel the magic around us intensifying, the air crackling with energy. Satan growled, holding onto the wound I had given him, it growing with each word of Latin Millie yelled.

"Michael!" she cried, "Strike now!"

Michael's wings flattered open and burst upward, the light of his wings glowing, his sword raised above his head. He brought it down with a force that seemed to split the Earth, aiming for Satan's flaming blade. The two swords collided, and there was a flash so bright it blinded me for a moment, much like our encounter with Belphegor.

When my vision cleared, I saw Satan stumbling, his sword flickering like a dying flame. But he wasn't yet beaten, no, not even close.

Satan snarled, and the ground around him cracked, his once handsome figure now turning smaller and one of a hideous creature with black eyes and sharp teeth. He raised his fists, summoning a wall of fire that rushed towards us with terrifying speed.

"Flynn!" Millie shouted. "Get back!"
I leaped aside just as the fire roared past us, the fire catching the side of my leg as I screeched out in pain, Millie grabbing

my hand and pulling me over to her fire, away from the fire. I lifted my pant leg to see that I had been burned pretty badly, tears forming in my eyes.

"Are you okay!?" Millie asked in a panic, trying to help me while also trying to recite her ancient spells as Micheal distracted the demon.

"Yeah, I'm- I'm okay! Keep going!" I replied, trying to stand up, shifting my weight to my other leg as I grabbed my dagger and held it tight. Millie nodded, looking like she wanted to do more to help, but she knew she couldn't. Her hands moved in a way that showed exact precision, and her face stayed firm, but I could tell from her eyes that she was beginning to get drained from the power usage.

I knew I needed to do something- anything- to shift the battle in our favor. I closed my eyes for a split second, reaching deep within myself, searching for the divine spark I felt just moments ago, praying, begging for a response from God. The power of the saints was within me; I just needed to find it, and I had to wield it like a weapon. I felt it there, deep down- a well of light and strength waiting to be drunk from.

I opened my eyes, and the dagger in my hand began to glow brighter, the divine energy within it responding to my call. I could feel the power flowing through my blood, making me feel lighter, stronger, faster. I focused on that power and that feeling and was ready to use it to turn the tide. "Millie!" I shouted, "Get ready!"

She nodded, understanding instantly. "Just tell me when!"

I charged forward yet again, the light from the dagger cutting through the darkness and smoke that had begun to surround Satan like a wall. Satan's eyes narrowed, and he swung his flaming sword at me, but this time I was ready. I ducked under the swing and drove the dagger up and into his side.

There was another flash of light, brighter this time, and Satan howled in pain, genuine pain, his form getting smaller again like a dying flame. "Now, Millie!" I yelled.

Millie's hands moved rapidly, her voice rising in the Latin chant, the words seeming to shake the world. The ancient spell was a song, a song of light and power that resonated in my bones. I felt Satan's strength weaken, his dark power faltering even more, leaving as quickly as water leaves a broken glass, as soon as time goes sneaking by.

Michael seized the moment. With a cry of defiance, he soared upwards again, his wings a blur, and came crashing down with his sword aimed straight at Satan's temple. The blade met its mark, slicing through the demon's head drawing a golden light across Satan's blackened skin.

Satan roared, a sound that made the ground shake, but fear was now in his eyes. "You think this changes anything!? You can't defeat them; you can't beat *him*!" He bellowed. "You are all just entertainment for him. Mark my words, Chosen One, you can't beat him. No one will conquer our master, **Damian**!"

Before I could ask any questions, the power that coursed through me grew more assertive. I had felt this power throughout my journey, but now I thought it wanted to be released. I was hesitant to use it, afraid it wouldn't work, that I wasn't worthy, that I'd fail. But I knew I couldn't hold back when I stood in the face of danger.

I took a deep breath and closed my eyes softly, feeling the power build. In a single focused burst, I let the power out. I thrust the dagger forward, and a beam of light so beautiful, a beam of pure light, shot from the blade, slamming directly into Satan's chest. He screamed, a sound that shook even the heavens, which were no longer the saint's land.

Millie's chant still grew louder, her voice rising into a war cry, a scream. I could see the strain on her face; the effort to keep the spell going exhausted her. "Hold on, Millie!" I shouted, feeling the strain in my voice.

"I've got this," she gritted out, sweat pouring down her face, yet she smiled at me.

Satan stumbled, his flames supporting like a flickering light. "This cannot be," he growled. "He will kill you; he is power! He is the storm! He is-"

"He is nothing," I interrupted, my voice filled with newfound confidence. "He is just another obstacle, another test. Just like you."

I charged again, my dagger blazing like a star. Satan swung his sword wildly, but his movements were slower, less confident. I dodged his attacks with ease, each step bringing me closer, each swipe of my dagger weakening him further.

Michael was relentless, his sword flashing in the dim light as he struck again and again, forcing Satan back toward the side of a mountain. "Flynn, we're wearing him down!" Michael, he called, a grin breaking across his face.

Satan's fury was evident, his eyes voids of nothingness. "You think you can defeat me?" he roared. "I will show you true power!"

He raised his hands, and the ground itself convulsed. Columns of fire arose from the Earth, jagged rocks splitting the air like the world was being torn apart. "Millie!" I shouted, "Can you stop this?"

"I'm trying!" She yelled back, her hands waving through the air faster than I could follow. "He's too strong!"
But I could feel it—the divine power inside of me, still waiting, growing. I knew what I had to do. I raised the dagger above my head, focusing all my will and strength on the blade. The light flared, blinding and searing, as I brought it down with all my might into the ground.

A shockwave of pure divine light bursts forth, cutting through the fire as if it were nothing, extinguishing it immediately, and shattering the rocks mid-air. A rock hit Satan square in the chest, and he cried out again in pain, looking as though he was being pulled apart from the inside.

"Now, Michael!" I screamed.

Michael shot forward like a missile, his sword blazing with holy light, and drove it straight into Satan's heart. There was a moment of silence—a heartbeat where everything seemed to stop. The air itself held its breath.

Then, with a final earth-shaking roar, Satan exploded into black liquid, smoke coming from the liquid. The liquid soon dissolved into nothing; the smell from the once-there liquid stayed, a scent of death that made me gag.

Millie collapsed to her knees, gasping for breath, her hands trembling from maintaining the spell. Micheal landed beside her, his wings holding around himself protectively, his sword glowing faintly in his hand.

I stood there, panting, the dagger still in my grip, the light slowly fading from the blade. The empty land was silent, the air still, and for a moment, I felt a sense of peace, of calm.

"We did it," I whispered, almost afraid to believe it.

Michael nodded, a grin breaking across his face. "Yeah, you little shit, we did."

Millie looked up, her face weary up triumphant. "That was... intense," she said with a smile, her face flushed. "But it's over. We won."

"It's not over yet. We still have to face Lucifer and destroy that machine, but I know we can do it," I said with a smile, feeling a wave of exhaustion coming over me. We were close; our journey was almost over.

Somewhere in The Core...

The demons all around panicked; the children were just one ring of hell away from the Core, and if they could defeat

Lucifer and Damian, everything would be over, and they'd destroy the Core, freeing the saints.

Lucifer sat next to Damian, their eyes wide and their mouth agape as they watched Satan, Lucifer's brother, go down so quickly. "We need to make a plan; they are strong," Lucifer said with a hint of panic in his voice.

Damian's eyes met Lucifer's, his expression stoic. "I can't have you face them alone. They will easily defeat you and then me. We should face them both at the same time. If we combine our abilities, we can easily defeat them. I will not let Flynn defeat all I've worked for." Domain said, his voice laced with frustration.

"What?" Lucifer began, his eyebrows furrowed. "How do you know his name? Have you met before?"

"He's my fucking son."

Chapter Ten

The three of us hiked up the mountain we had cornered Satan against, and in the distance, I saw for the first time in five years what the world looked like before all Hell broke loose. There were trees, grass, cars, and everything before the catastrophic event. I felt my eyes begin to water just looking at it. Our journey was finally almost over.

In the center of all the beauty was the Core. It was a lot different from what I had imagined it to look like. It was a huge building constructed over a black river, and bubbles slowly floated to the top. You could see the heat waves coming off from the top of the dark liquid, and the building above glowed from electricity, something we in the Safe Haven didn't and possibly would never have. Seeing how close we were, I wanted to run up there and destroy the machine, but Millie was exhausted, and Michael was too. All of us needed to take a breather and make a plan.

I couldn't help but think about the name that kept being mentioned: *Damian*. God had mentioned the name, and now Satan had, too. Had he been the man who built the Core? I thought back to my mother the day my life flipped. She said she knew this day would come. She also warned me about a man with the initials D.W. Was that who she was referring to?

Who was he?

My thoughts were soon interrupted by Millie grabbing onto my hand. My face flushed red from the sudden touch, but it went down again quickly.

"We need to make a plan, but we should rest first," Millie said, her eyebrows furrowed and her face a bright red, probably from the battle we had just won.

I nodded, and Millie held my hand as she led me over to where Michael was seated. Millie and I plopped onto the hot ground, Michael stretching and massaging his wings. "We need to make a plan. Lucifer won't be easy to face," he said, his eyes narrowing in frustration as sweat trickled down his face.

"Who is Damian?" I questioned finally, messing with the strap of my bag. The question was eating me alive, and if anyone knew, it had to be Michael.

Michael just paused, and his eyes locked onto mine. "Damian? Who told you that name?"

"Satan said earlier in the battle that we were just his pawns, and in a dream, God came to me, and he mentioned him as well. He talked about facing him, I think." I answered with a shrug.

Michael's face went pale, and his eyes widened a bit. "He, *what??*" He said, his body jerking back a little.

"What? Who is he?" Millie asked as well, leaning into Micheal a bit.

"He's the one that made the damn Core," Micheal growled, his face scrunching up. "I didn't know we'd be facing him. I've never even *seen* him."

I felt my muscles tense up when Michael mentioned he was the one who made the Core. He was a mortal being, a scientist, who made a deal with the Devil and made the machine that converted energy into black magic, the reason Lucifer was so strong now. I didn't know much about him; honestly, no one dared to mention his name in the Safe Haven.

Michael's head fell into the palms of his hand, and surprisingly, he began to laugh. He laughed, shaking his head and holding it in his head. "We are so fucked." He said with a laugh. Millie and I exchanged glances, and I could see the fear on her face as well. She softly placed her black rotting hand on top of mine, attempting to comfort the both of us.

"We really need a plan," Michael said, shaking his head still.

So, the three of us brainstormed, eventually creating a two-step plan. It would start with Michael using his divine power to attempt to disguise himself as a servant of Lucifer, altering his appearance to look like one of a sinner. Flynn and Millie would also do this, Millie not needing to worry about it as much as her hands had already begun to rot with sin, so there wasn't much to disguise.

We'd then face Damian. I would take Damian on head first, using my dagger and newly found divine power against him. Hopefully, this will be strong enough to at least get us to the machine, which Millie would then use her incantations on as I would protect her, taking on anyone who'd get in our way.

Michael would continue deeper into the Core, finding and luring Lucifer away from the machine. Lucifer would likely sense this destruction, but it'll be too late when Michael's true identity is revealed. Michael would use all his skills and angelic power against him, Millie, and me, breaking the machine.
After the machine is destroyed, the saints will be free from their internal suffering and take control of the world, restoring peace to the universe once and for all.

The three of us began to prepare for the battle. Michael and I trained together, working on my reflexes as Millie worked on her incantations. We worked until the natural light disappeared, leaving the sky black, the only illumination from the Core. Seeing the Core so close to us just motivated me even more.

I was ready to face the final challenge.

Finally, we decided to take a break. I distributed the last remaining water in my bag as Michael gathered dirt, ready to eat. I reached into my bag and pulled out the loaf of forgotten bread, and Michael took gulps of the boiling dirt.

"Are you serious," Michael said, his eyes fixated on the loaf of bread I held. "I have been eating fucking dirt, and you have a loaf of bread!?" He yelled, tossing the dort he was eating to the side. Millie, amused at the sight, chuckled.

"I forgot I had this! Here!" I laughed, handing a piece of bread to Michael, who immediately grabbed it, shoving it down his throat. I passed a piece to Millie, who looked like she'd pee herself from laughing so hard at Michael.

I ate the final piece of bread, trying to eat it slowly but devouring it immediately despite my attempts.
We all told each other stories of our lives before the end. Millie talked about how she always was with her family,

working as soon as she turned ten. Michael lived peacefully alongside God, often taunting Lucifer. They had a lot of history, and Michael hated him. I talked about my mom. I spoke about how her hair would always frizz up, even after straightening it. How crinkled lines around her eyes would appear when she saw something she liked, how she would read Ness and I the bible, making sure we knew every verse and every passage.

All of us had such different lives before everything went down. We were happy.

After telling our stories, we decided to go to bed, preparing for tomorrow.

Somewhere in The Core...

Damian and Lucifer watched and listened intensely to our plan.

"So," Damian began, *"they plan on breaking in with a disguise? You know what, let them."*

"What? Why? Aren't you nervous they'll break the machine?" Lucifer questioned, his face wrinkling in concern.

"No," Damian replied, a smile forming on his face. *Don't worry; if he is anything like me, he won't be able to fight me. We'll be fine; maybe I can convince him to join me. Imagine his divine power mixed with my dark power—a recipe for success!"*

Lucifer let out a sharp exhale, shaking his head. He wanted to disagree, but he knew any attempt to do so would end in a screaming fit like two toddlers, so he just turned around and left. Damian continued staring at the screen, smiling and wide-eyed, watching me.

"Welcome home, Flynn."

Chapter Eleven

The three of us began to prepare to infiltrate the Core. Michael hid his wings in his hoodie, smearing dirt over his cuts to make them look rotten. Millie and I sat off to the side, watching the light from the Core. Millie helped me wrap a torn piece of my shirt around my leg. It still hurt, but it had gotten better since yesterday.

The two of us sat there, a bittersweet moment. Our journey was almost over, but I couldn't help but feel sad. I had met old friends, and considering there was no known way to reverse the power of the seven deadly sins corrupting your soul, Millie was bound to turn into just another blood-thirsty sinner indeed. Hopefully, when we'd free the saints, they'd know how to save her soul and reverse the damage.

"I'm scared, Flynn," Millie spoke in a low whisper. I looked over at her with a confused expression, and she continued. "What comes after all this? It's been so long since I've had a genuine everyday life. It scares me to think what it'll be like."

I nodded and sighed, looking back over to the Core. It was scary. After years of living in the Safe Haven, a tiny spot in the middle of nowhere, we'd now have the whole world to roam. How do you even function like that? In a way, I didn't want to leave the Safe Haven. The world was so big, and I wanted to stay in my space with the people who loved me, yet I knew I had to finish this, not for myself but for everyone else's future.

Michael came over to the two of us. "Are you two ready yet? If we want to pull this off, we should go now." Millie and I shared exchanges before nodding and standing up.

"Yeah," I said, my face filled with determination as I gripped my bag that had my blessed dagger in. "Let's do this." Millie nodded, too, and we began to walk towards the Core.
Michael explained how he would fly us there, but that would blow his cover of being a demon and all. On our way there, we all walked with our chests out and heads up, giving subtle nods to the demons we passed. Confidence was vital; that's what my mother always told me, and she was right.
Soon, we made it to the building. There were many demons, some working, some eating, and others just hanging out. It was like a mall for demons. It was weird seeing creatures other than sinners; you could tell the difference. Sinners were violent, hissed, and often acted in an animalistic way. Demons, however, acted much more human. They talked usually, weren't violent to each other, and worked.

The three of us found signs littered around the building, showing where to go to the Core. It was all too easy. Soon, we got into a packed elevator, getting squished into the back. We all shared nervous glances.

"One of you guys needs to take a shower!" Yelled a random demon in the front, sniffing the air. "You smell like a human, and you know the boss hates that smell!"

I felt my face go pale, and my eyes widen. We were literally being sniffed out. Micheal tried subtly standing closer to a demon, attempting to get some of their smells onto him. Millie and I followed what he did, hoping to get even the littlest smell of demon onto us. Soon, it reached our floor, the Core's floor. Most of the other demons got off on the cafeteria floor, so only two others got off at the Core. This was the perfect time to attack.

Michael separated from us and followed the signs to Lucifer's office while Millie and I went in the other direction, locating the machine. Michael soon found Lucifer. He was seated atop a throne of bones and rubies, shadows around him moving like humans. His eyes were red, and he was gorgeous. He wore a cocky, prideful expression and a black suit. His black hair was slicked back, his body had a perfect buffness, and his suit perfectly showed it off.

Millie and I followed the signs to the machine, quickly finding it. It was made of dark, firm metal, with satanic symbols carved onto it that glowed and pulsated. You could feel the energy coming off of it, the dark power. Millie began to prepare herself, her eyes closing as her hands moved in a delicate motion, and she began to whisper some ancient Latin that I couldn't comprehend.

Meanwhile, Lucifer recognizes Michael immediately, giving him a sinister smile. "Oh, my love, you came back!" Lucifer says with a smirk, standing up from his throne. Michael closes and locks the door to the prince's office behind him.

"I'm not your 'love,' Luci," Michael replied, crossing his arms and rolling his eyes.

"Awe!" Lucifer smiled, "still calling me 'Luci?' How cute!"

Michael just rolled his eyes. Calling Lucifer "Luci" had become a habit to piss off the demon, but for some reason, he liked it. "Just don't," Micheal scoffed. "I'm here to beat your ass for locking me and everyone else in Hell. Like damn, you locked your dad down there, you're an asshole." Micheal growled, his wings expanding, pulling out the sword from Belphegor.

Lucifer laughed, his eyes glowing and his palms beginning to turn a rotten black. "I've heard that one before, baby." He said with a smirk as Micheal lunged towards him.

I kept guard, ensuring no demons entered the room while Millie recited her ancient incantation. She continued her spell, her voice rising the more words she'd say. I looked around anxiously, gripping my bag so tight my knuckles turned white. I knew I had to face Damian, where was he?

Suddenly, out of the shadows, a man appeared.

"You really thought it'd be that easy?" The man taunted, his eyes dark and flashing. I tried to reach for my dagger, but it was too late. The man began to recite a spell, and before I could do anything, I felt a sudden cold and eerie sensation. The room started to spin, and my senses were confused. I could smell perfume, see flashing lights of different colors, feel the air against my skin, taste a rotten flavor from the wind, and hear laughter, not just any laughter, but laughter from a woman I had faced earlier in my journey.

Then I saw her. It was Lilith. She kept appearing and disappearing. I tried to close my eyes, but when I did, I saw visions of my mother, visions of her mangled corpse, bleeding out as her organs splattered across the ground, her eyes rolled back and her mouth agape. I turned away from Lilith and heard screaming, a familiar scream, ***Ness's screams.***

I looked toward the screams and saw Ness being turned apart, starting from toes and fingers. He was being torn apart from the man I had just seen emerge from the shadows. I understood now that he was the one everyone was warning me about. This was **Damian.** I watched Ness's blood squirt out everywhere, him calling for me, begging me to save him. I closed my eyes again, now seeing my mother being eaten off the ground by white-eyed demons, taking bites out of her as she screamed and cried.

I turned back forward, Lilith now running at my full speed. She was screaming at me in Latin, screeching.

You're the reason they're all here!

Lilith yelled.

You're the reason they'll all die!

I pulled out my dagger and, in one firm motion, plunged my blade right into her heart. Immediately, her voice was gone, and she began to cough up blood, it getting on my shirt as her eyes filled with tears. The visions then stopped. I was back in the Core, in front of the machine, showing me something even more terrifying. I regained my senses, seeing Millie with my blade in her chest.

Millie gasped, and I realized the blood Lilith was coughing up onto me was actually Millie's, her blood soaking my shirt as she screamed and cried, trying to take the dagger out of her chest weakly. Her eyes filled with fear, confusion, and hurt, and she looked at me, tears falling down the sides of her face.

"Why...?" Millie mutters, looking at me betrayed, the blood dripping down her chin and staining her teeth and lips as she collapses onto the cold floor, her body twitching as she dies. I screamed, a gutting scream, as I got on my knees next to her, not caring that my skin and clothes would be stained with her blood. My hands shook, and my body tensed up, seeing what I had done.

Seeing her dead body, I began to gag and throw up beside her as I sobbed. It felt like someone had punched me in the gut as I watched the puddle of blood form underneath her lifeless body. Damian watched all this from the shadows, smiling as he watched me panic, trying to do anything to wake her.

In the midst of the fight Michael and Lucifer were engaged in, he heard my scream and, knowing something was wrong, screamed out for me. He rushes over to the machine where I am, my sobs and screams filling the air.

"Flynn!" Michael screams, "Get ahold of yourself!" He says before seeing the body of the once-determined girl lying on the ground in a puddle of blood, the dagger belonging to me sticking out of her chest.

Michael, seeing the sight, becomes enraged and rushes to Damian, who is watching, eyes full of malice. However, Lucifer has been waiting for this moment; he spreads his black feathered wings and soars up at incredible speed in one big push. He suddenly appears in front of Michael, punching his gut in one swift movement and force, the angel falling to the ground due to the impact.

Lucifer grabs Michael by the wings and tears the wings from the archangel in one decisive movement. The sound of the tear fills the room. It goes silent momentarily as the loud pop and tears creep into everyone's ears like spiders.
Immediately, golden blood squirts and floods over the angel's back. He lets out a deep guttural scream, using his hands to try to feel where his wings where his wings once used to be.

Michael collapses to the ground, screaming and crying at the pain as Lucifer throws his wings to the side with a piece of garbage. The eyes of the angel dim, his screams filling the room as I freeze, unable to move or react, just staring in fear and disbelief. Lucifer laughs, plunging his hand into the wound, making Michael scream louder, the sound echoing through the building. "Always too quick to rush into the fray without thinking," Lucifer says with a smile, his hand in the wound where the angel's wings used to be, beginning to twist his hand.

Michael screams and cries, trying to stand up, but Lucifer kicks him down again, his jaw banging against the metal floor. Lucifer then waves his hand, a cage forming from underneath Michael. The bars are black, pulsating with dark energy, spikes on the bottom, constantly stabbing Michael as he lets out deep screams and sobs of pain.
"It's a shame us angels can't die. I guess you'll have to pray for death for all of eternity now as you watch the little 'Chosen One' fail and *die*." Lucifer taunts Michael, still screaming, crying, and shaking his head.

I sit there in shock, my eyes wide, my hands that are covered still in Millie's blood clasped over my mouth as I sob. Damian takes a step closer to me and squats down next to me, using his hand to move my head so I can look at him. I am too terrified to fight back against his touch.

"Oh, Flynn," Damian begins, smiling as he runs his fingers through my hair. "I've waited so long for this moment." He says softly, almost tenderly.

My eyes scan his face, his soft expression; confused, I manage to stutter out one word: *"What..."* I say, tears continuing down my cheeks, my hands staining my mouth and face with the blood of my friend.

"Didn't you ever wonder why you were chosen? Why do you wield the power you do?" Damian asks, his voice dripping with malice, his breath hot against my face. "It's because of me. *I am your father, Flynn.* The darkness flows through your veins, mixed with the divine. That's why you are… special."

I recoil, my face filled with horror and disgust. "No…" I say in disbelief. "You're lying, that's not true!" I snap myself out of my trance by his words, scooting back away from him, but I am put back into my trance as I hurry back too far, hitting Millie's body.

"Oh, it's true." Damian sneers. "Your mother— she tried to keep you away from me, tried to hide you in the light of the holy. But darkness calls to darkness, my son. And now, you've taken your first step in embracing your true heritage."

My mind reels from the revelation, a storm of emotions swirling inside me. "No… I won't believe it! I'm nothing like you!" I yell, beginning to pull out my hair from the stress and panic.

Damian chuckles. "Oh, but you are! You just killed your friend, my boy. That's just the beginning. Join me, and we can learn what you are truly capable of." He says, outstretching his hand to me.

My heart pounds in my chest, sweat pouring down my face, stinging my eyes. Fear, anger, and despair all flood my body,

I know that if I couldn't take down the two with the help of an angel, I couldn't do it myself, especially after what I had just done. I look to my side, seeing Michael caged and unconscious, bleeding. The weight of the failure is too much.

As Damian begins to close in, I back up, hitting the body of my friend once again. Overwhelmed and fearful, I see an opening to escape. I grab my dagger, closing my eyes and gagging as I pull it out of Millie's chest, gathering all my strength, trying to plague all of my remaining divine power and put it into the blade like the fight with Satan. I use my energy to slam the dagger into the ground. This creates a bright light, momentarily blinding the two men as I take my chance and run. I dash through the walls of the Core, finding a flight of stairs and taking them instead of the elevator. I don't look back. I leave the building, running across the mountain as fast as possible.

Lucifer goes to the balcony of the building, his laugh echoing through the vast landscape, Damian by his side, watching as I, his son, run. "Run, little chosen one!" Lucifer calls after me teasingly. "Run and remember this day— the day you killed your friend and the day you and your God failed."

Damian watched me closely, smiling as I ran. "Let him run," he says. "He'll come back. They always do... Especially when they want vengeance."

I slumped against a tree on the other side of the mountain and sobbed. I sobbed for Millie, I cried for Michael, and I sobbed for everyone I let down. I couldn't forget the face Millie made when my blade stuck deep into her chest and Michael's scream; it all plagued my thoughts—days passed before I even left the tree, weak and tired. I hadn't slept those days; two things filled my mind: despair and **vengeance.**

I only had one idea on how to do this: the saints from the **Safe Haven.**

Chapter Twelve

The world had grown seemingly darker since my disappearance. Two years had passed since the day I fled, broken and scared, leaving my lone alive friend in the shadow of defeat. Damian, the man who claimed to be my father, had shattered my spirit with the revelation that drowned his soul. Millie, my closest ally, lay dead by my own hands, tricked by my father's dark magic. Michael, the archangel, remained imprisoned, his wings severed, his light dimmer. Lucifer, the fallen one, continued his reign, the machine still running, keeping God under control.

The world continued to be overcast with clouds of ash and smoke, the air heavy with despair. People no longer ventured outside the Safe Haven to fix the madness but prayed for death. All hope was lost, and their savior had failed.

But one day, something changed. A figure appeared outside the Safe Haven, a human. Not just any human, me, Flynn. I was the first person to cross back over through the barrier of Safe Haven, my soul free of the stain of sin, and now I had one purpose: train these remaining men and women for the fight of their lives, a revolution against Lucifer and Damian.

The air was thick with tension as I surveyed the camp. I had led the saints to the open field where I previously fought Satan. It was an easy journey now that I had killed six of the seven deadly sins, only leaving Lucifer. The saints gathered here were no warriors; they were humanity's last hope, soldiers of the divine preparing to march against the greatest evil the world had ever known.

For two years, I had been haunted by the memories of that terrible day: the sound of Millie taking her final breath, the sight of Michael's wings being severed and his body caged, and the revelation of Damian's dark parentage. I had run then, but I would not run this time. I was the Chosen One, wielding the power of the divine God and the blessed dagger, and I vowed to return when the day was exemplary.

Today was that day.

Ness, my younger brother, stood beside me. He was no longer the wide-eyed boy he had been when I left; he had grown into a warrior in his own right. Over the past two years, Ness had trained relentlessly, proving that time and time again, he wasn't just Flynn's little brother.

"We've gathered as many saints as we could," Ness said, his voice steady even though he was eleven, his eyes scanning the camp. "Fifty of us, ready to follow you."

I nodded, my gaze sweeping over the camp. Saints of all kinds were here, some dressed in armor, some just in simple robes, all of them littered with deep battle scars that they obtained in the journey here, constantly being attacked by the hungry sinners of Hell; some even losing small body parts like fingers or even hands or arms. All the saints bared the same undeniable divine light. They all brought their weapons, blessed by a pastor, before leaving the small refuge we called home. They were all here because they believed in me; they believed that together, we could free the world from Lucifer's grasp.

I turned to my brother, a faint smile across my lips. "You've done so well, Ness. I couldn't have done any of this without you."

Ness grinned. "You'd better not forget that when this is all over."

I chuckled softly, my heart lighter for a moment, but then remembered what was to come, the weight of what lay ahead pressing down on him. "Let's gather everyone. It's time to speak."

Ness and I were soon gathered around by the saints, all eager to hear what my brother and I had to say. Faces young and old, eyes full of dread and determination, stared back at me. I took a deep breath and began.

"Two years," I said, my voice clear and strong. "It's been two long years since I've last faced Lucifer and Damian. Since we've lost Millie and Michael is being held captive, we've been in hiding, gathering our strength and preparing for this moment. And now, we're ready."

I paused, letting the words sink in, then continued, "We have a plan. We know what we must do, but I won't lie; this won't be easy. This will be the most complex challenge of your life, and some of you may not make it back. Just remember why you are here now and what we stand for."

A murmur ran through the crowd, a mixture of fear and determination. I could see their resolve strengthening, their hearts steeling for what lay ahead.

Ness stepped forward, his voice rising with the same intensity. "We have one shot to do this right —Lucifer's machine— the one that gives the sinners and demons their dark abilities. We must destroy this machine and Damian, allowing the saints to retake world control."

I nodded, speaking up after my brother. "We strike at dawn. We move quickly and quietly, catching them off guard. Our goal is to rescue Michael and destroy that machine. With God's power on our side, we will prevail."

A cheer rose from the crowd, initially quiet but growing in intensity. I could feel the fire igniting their beliefs, which also helped ignite mine. I raised my hand, the camp falling silent again. "Tonight, we prepare. Check your weapons, say your prayers, and be ready for what's to come. We fight as one — for Michael, Millie, and the world."

After the speech, the camp buzzed with activity. Ness and I moved among the saints, checking weapons, distributing supplies, and giving words of encouragement. I stopped by a young group of saints who were sharpening their blades.

"Keep your blades light and fast," I advised, calm but authoritative. "Lucifer and Damian are swift and relentless; he'll also have his minions with him. You need to strike and move, not staying in one place for too long."

Ness was nearby, instructing a group of archers. "Remember, the machine is heavy duty and will probably be heavily guarded. Look for the sigils that mark their bindings to Lucifer — hit those, and they should fall faster."
I watched my brother, pride swelling in my chest. Ness had grown into a leader in his own right, fierce and determined. When I initially left two years ago, I would've never brought him along into battle, but now I couldn't imagine doing it without him.

Across the ca,p, a group of saints gathered around Mr. Evans, one of the older saints who had been training his ancient spells and studying them ever since I had left. I joined them, listening as he explained the enchantments they'd use to counteract Damian's dark powers, teaching the saints who listened to him.

"Damian and his minions will try to overwhelm us with sheer force," Mr. Evans said, his voice calm and confident. "But the spells I have been teaching you will weaken them and their connection to the dark power. Remember your training. Trust in the light."

I nodded in agreement. "Well said, Mr. Evans. Stay close together. Your spells will be our best defense against their magic."

As preparations continued, I found a quiet spot in the corner of the camp. I just needed a moment to think and pray. I closed my eyes, feeling the weight of the upcoming battle upon my shoulders.

Two years. Two long years of waiting, planning, training, and hoping for this moment. I could feel God's power resonate within me, the strength that carried me this far, but I could also feel fear. It was the fear of failure, losing more people I cared about, and not being strong enough. I was the Chosen One, but I was still just a man.

I took a deep breath, closing my eyes softly. "God," I whispered, "give me strength and courage. Help me lead them through this."

A rustling of leaves behind me made me turn. Ness was there, watching him with a knowing smile. "Praying?"

I nodded with a smile. "Always."

Ness came closer, sitting down beside me. "You've got this, Flynn. You've been through worse."

I chuckled. "I hope you're right, Ness."

Ness grinned. "Of course I am. I always am."

My smile faded slightly, replaced by a more severe expression. "You've grown a lot, Ness—more than I could have imagined. I'm proud of you."

Ness looked down, emotion flickering in his eyes. "Thanks, Flynn. I wouldn't be here without you. And I know... I know this will be hard, but I'm ready. We're all ready."

I nodded, feeling a surge of confidence from my brother's voice. "We'll do this together. For Millie, for Michael, for everyone."

As the last day faded, I called the saints together again. They gathered in a circle around me. I looked around and saw the faces of all these people, my people, my friends.

"Tonight, we rest," I began. Tomorrow, we fight. Remember, our mission has two steps: rescue Michael and break the machine. Stay focused, stay together. We move quickly and strike hard. This is our chance to end this once and for all."

I turned to face Mr. Evans and the other older saints. "You'll lead the first group, focusing on any minor demons that'll try to stop us. Ness, you're with me — we're heading straight for the machine."

Ness nodded, his jaw set with determination. "We'll take them by surprise."

I continued, "Remember, they will use every trick they have to break our spirit. Don't let them. Stay strong in your faith, trust each other, and trust in the light of God."

Silence fell over the camp as the saints took in my words. Then, they began to pray one by one. Their voices started as a quiet hum but rose softly, filling the empty night sky. I closed my eyes, letting the strength and faith their voices carried wash over me and surround me like a warm embrace,

I knew they were ready.

They would face their greatest challenge tomorrow, yet they would fight like their lives depended on it because it did. And this time, Flynn would not run.

As the camp grew into a restless quiet, Ness and I sat atop the mountain, looking over the Core like I had done with Millie and Michael those years ago. I felt a deep calm settle over me, a certainty that I was on the right path. I looked over to my brother, and for a moment, I saw not a seasoned warrior, but the younger brother I had always longed to protect.

"Do you ever get scared, Flynn?" Ness asked suddenly, his voice soft as the light from the Core illuminated his face, allowing me to see his long hair resting on his shoulders.

I considered the question, then nodded. "All the time, dude," I said with a chuckle. "But I've learned that courage isn't about not being afraid; it's about continuing despite fear."

Ness smiled. "Then I guess I'm courageous, too."

I laughed quietly, reaching over to ruffle my younger brother's hair. "More than you know, dude. More than you know."

As we sat together, watching the illuminated Core from across the mountain, I felt the weight of the past two years lift, even if just a little.

The camp grew quieter by the second as the night wore on, and the saints found sleep. I stayed awake, my eyes on the horizon, waiting for the first light of dawn.

Tomorrow, they would fight.
Tomorrow, they would win.

Somewhere in The Core...

"You know," Damian began. "Today marks the second anniversary since we've seen that boy."

Lucifer nodded, looking up from the machine he had been running his fingers along, the energy from the machine slowly flowing into his bloodstream. "Yes, I am aware. I thought he'd come back, but there hasn't been any sign of him in two years. Maybe we truly are free of him." He said with a shrug, looking at the machine.

"No," Damian turned to face Lucifer, his face cold and stern. He will come back. Deep down, he knows he is just like

me, full of hate and vengeance. It's just a matter of time until he gives in."

Chapter Thirteen

Suddenly, a bright light appeared in the sky, falling down onto the ground. It wasn't like the light from the Core; it was not artificial; it was natural, genuine sunlight. The soldiers of Lucifer, his legions of demons and corrupted souls, looked up in confusion. Their slitted eyes narrowed, unaccustomed to such brightness. Whispers spread among them, anxious murmurs vibrating through their rank.

Lucifer's voice broke the silence, powerful and resonant, accompanied by Damian. "Do you feel that?" Lucifer asked, his almond-shaped eyes narrowing at the light and his suit glistening with a nasty sheen. "Something's coming… something—"

A figure suddenly appeared on the other side of the mountain facing the Core, the silhouette blazing with divine intent. It was me. I stepped with a thunderous impact, my feet planting firmly on the dried, broken ground. I wore the battle-scarred armor of a warrior, my eyes alight with determination. I held my blessed dagger in my hand, the blade shimmering with an ethereal glow.

Behind me, a variety of figures followed, descending behind me like angels of the divine. Each one was dressed differently—in robes, armor, or even just shirts and pants—

yet they shimmered with celestial power. The small army of saints, warriors blessed by God, stood at my side, their expressions fierce and determined.

Lucifer's forces recoiled, and a murmur of disbelief rippled through the building. "It's him," one whispered. The Chosen One has returned.

I raised my voice, clear and commanding, echoing across the vast landscape. "Lucifer! Damian! I have come to finish what we started. I have come to end your reign of terror and free the world from your darkness!"

There was a pause—a heartbeat of silence. Then, laughter. Cold, mocking laughter echoed from the tallest tower of the fortress. Lucifer emerged outside the building, his eyes burning with malice as his dark wings spread wide. Beside him stood Damian, a smirk playing at the corner of his lips.

"Flynn," Lucifer sneered, his voice a low growl. "I wondered when you'd crawl back. Two years hiding in the shadows, and now you think you can challenge me with this… pitiful excuse of an army?"

My gaze hardened. "I have returned with the light of fifty saints by my side. I have come to end this, once and for all."

Lucifer's eyes flicked to Damian. "What do you think, Damian? Shall we humor the boy?"

Damian's eyes widened, a sinister light dancing in his eyes. "Let's see what he has learned in his absence."

Lucifer nodded. "So be it. But make no mistake, Flynn—you and your army will die today; the offer to join us went off the table two years ago."

Lucifer smirked, and with a snap of his hands, demons surged forward, a wave of darkness and hatred, their weapons gleaming in the light. The saints stood their ground, forming a small line of defense, their swords and other weapons drawn, others preparing their incantations.

I held up my hand. "Hold the line! Do not let them break through!"

The saints, moving as one, formed a barrier, the saints reciting ancient incantations that pushed back against the encroaching darkness.

I turned to my brother, who held a sword, his eyebrows furrowed and confused. "Are you ready?"

Ness, still untested but resolute, nodded. "I'm ready. We'll fight together."

My face softened for a brief moment. "Stay close, and remember— you have power, even if you don't know its full extent yet."

My brother nodded, gripping his sword tightly. "I won't let you down."

My voice cut through the air. "Saints! Charge!" I screamed, the noise seeming to rumble the ground.

And with that, the army of saints surged forward, meeting Lucifer and Damian's forces head-on. The battlefield exploded into chaos— a symphony of clashing swords, roaring demons, and the hiss of divine fire burning through corrupted flesh.

I moved like a cyclone, my blessed bagger flashing with divine light, cutting through demons and sinners with precision and power. I dodged a swing from a hulking brute, ducked under another's clumsy blow, and plunged my dagger deep into the throat of the third one, sending it howling back in pain.

I looked around, seeing my brother fight bravely beside me, deflecting attacks and striking with unexpected strength and speed. For someone so new to battle, he held his ground remarkably well, his face set with determination.

"Keep going forward!" I shouted, leaping forward to block a demon's blade aimed at my brother's back. I deflected the attack, spun, and, with a swift strike, decapitated the creature.

In the distance, I saw Damian as he watched the battle unfold with a calm, calculating gaze. I knew Damian would make his move soon, and once he did, I'd be prepared.

But for now, I fought, each strike driven by purpose, each motion a prayer for the lost and fallen. I felt the divine power coursing through me, felt the guidance of something greater than me, and for the first time in two years, I felt whole.

Yet, the battle raged on, relentless. The saints were fighting with all their force, but Lucifer's forces were vast and well-trained, and the darkness was merciless in its assault. I knew we could not win with sheer power alone. We needed another plan.

I quickly move towards a small group of saints, shouting above the screams of battle. "Form up around me! We need to push towards the machine! If we destroy it, we can break Lucifer's hold!"

The saints nodded, understanding immediately. They formed a wedge, me at the front, driving through the sea of demons, their light cutting through the darkness like a blade.

But as we neared the building and the machine, I felt a sudden chill run down my spine. I turned and saw Damian striding towards me, dark energy swirling around his hands. The crowd of demons parted for him as if sensing his evil power.

"Flynn!" Damian yelled out, his voice cutting through the chaos of war like a knife. "Face me!"

My jaw tightened, my eyes narrowing as I gripped my dagger tighter, my eyes never leaving the man. "This ends now, Damian."

Damian laughed, a cold, cruel sound. "Does it? I've worked for this for two years, son. To see if you return. To see if you'd embrace your nature."

I felt as the anger, my old doubt, all bubbled up inside me. "I am not your son. I am not your heir. I am Flynn, the righteous hand of God."

Damian's eyes glittered with dark amusement. "And I am your own personal Hell."

With a flick of the wrist, Damian sent a wave of dark energy surging towards me. I raised my dagger, channeling divine light to counter the attack. The two energies crashed in the air, sparkling and crackling, the ground beneath them trembling with force, making everyone else on the battlefield, including the demons, stop fighting.

I pushed back, feeling the strength of God behind me, feeling the power of his will, his faith, his power. I took another step forward, then another, forcing Damian back.

But Damian was more potent, more robust than I had remembered. And there was something else, something dark and insidious that lurked beneath his power, something that whispered to me to call out the darkness within my blood.

Damian smiled. "You feel it, don't you? The pull of darkness? You can't deny what you are, Flynn. You can't deny your heritage.

I gritted my teeth, sweat rolling down my face. "I can, and I will."

With a roar, I surged forward, my blessed dagger glowing with holy light. I swung at Damian, who blocked me with a shield of dark energy. The two of us clashed, our powers glowing, trying to empower the other.

I felt the darkness whispering to me, trying to seep into my thoughts, my heart. But I pushed it back, focusing on the light, on my purpose, on the faces of those I cared for.

"You are not my father," I snarled, slashing at Damian's face.

Damian dodged, his smile never faltering. "But I am, Flynn. And I'm the only one who can teach you what you truly are."

I swung again, harder, faster, trying to silence my doubts, my fear. "I don't need you. I have the power of God on my side."

Damian laughed. "We shall see, Flynn. We shall see."

The battle between the father and son raged in, their powers colliding in a spectacle of light and shadow.

The battlefield trembled under the weight of the divine and infernal power clashing. The sound of steel striking against steel filled the air, mingled with the crackling fire and the cries of the wounded and the ones mourning the saints who'd died in battle. Even throughout all of this, though, the saints continued their valiant fight against Lucifer and his demonic forces, their light slicing through the shadow; the tide of darkness seemed endless. I could feel the tension in every muscle, every breath. My heart pounded with the rhythm of a thousand battle drums.

Damian's laughter echoed over the land, a low, mocking sound that cut through my focus like a jagged knife. "You still fight like a child, Flynn. There is so much power in you— so much potential. If only you'd accept what you are, this battle would be over already."

My grip tightened around the hilt of my blessed dagger. "I am what I choose to be, Damian. I won't be the puppet you wanted."

Damian's smirk widened, his eyes gleaming with a mixture of amusement and malice. "I admire your stubbornness, son. But this… this is where it ends."

With a swift motion, Damian unleashed a torrent of dark energy, a swirling vortex that hurled towards me like a living shadow. I barely had enough time to react, having to raise my blade unstably, channeling another blast of holy light to counter it.

I felt the strain in my arms, the weight of Damian's power pressing down against my own. For a moment, my mind drifted back to Millie's face— her laughter, her fierce determination, her trust in me. I could not let her death be in vain. I pushed harder, feeling the warmth of divine power from my core, through my veins, and into my blessed dagger.

The dark vortex began to waver, flickering like a dying light. I pushed forward, step by agonizing step, feeling the strength grow in every breath. Damian's expression shifted, his confidence faltering.

But just as the tide began to turn in my favor, a scream pierced the air— a scream I knew all too well. I turned my head, my heart dropping to my stomach. My brother, only a few yards away, was on his knees, bloody, surrounded by three demons who were closing in on him with sharp blades.

My breath caught in my throat. "NO!"

I broke away from Damian, his dark energy rushing into behind where I was, hitting the mountain behind us as Damian fell to his knees. My blade cut through the arm of a demon as I dashed to my brother's side. "Get away from him!" I shouted, my voice raw, dripping with panic.

Ness looked up at me, eyes wide, sweat dripping down his face. I could see the fear there, the uncertainty, but I could also see something else— something flickering beneath the surface, a spark, a glimmer of light I knew all too well. I then knew he didn't need my help, even if he himself thought he did.

"Use it!" I shouted. "Use the power inside you! You have it; I know you do!"

My brother swallowed, his grip on his sword tightening. "I... I don't know how!"

I blocked another attack; my movements were fluid and fast, but my voice remained somehow steady. "Trust yourself. Feel it, let it guide you."

Another group of demons lunged, but in an instant, I watched as my brother panicked, his eyes turning a glowing white. His body seemed to glow from the inside as if lit by an inner sun. He raised his sword and, with a shout, unleashed a wave of divine energy that blasted the demons back, disintegrating them into ash.

I grinned widely, my heart swelling with relief and happiness. "That's it! You did it!"

But there was no time for celebration. Seeing my brother's awakening, Damian closed the distance between them. "So, another child of mine has unlocked his true power," Damian sneered, raising a hand to cast a spell. "Let us see if you're as stubborn as your brother."

Before Damian could unleash his dark magic, I threw myself in front of Ness, raising my dagger. "You'll have to get through me first."

Damian's smile widened. "Gladly."

He thrust his hand forward, and a beam of dark energy erupted from his palm, aimed straight at me. I quickly swung my dagger, the blade flaring with holy light, meeting the dark beam again head-on.

Encouraged by his newfound power, Ness stepped up beside me, raising his sword. "Together!" he shouted.

I nodded, feeling a surge of energy from my brother, as if our powers were feeding off one another, intertwining like strands of light. We pushed together; our combined force was driving Damian back, his feet sliding across the dry ground and up against the building where the machine lay inside.

For the first time, I saw something other than pride flicker in Damian's eyes— uncertainty, maybe even fear. "NO!" Damian roared, his voice cracking with desperation. "You will not defeat me!"

But we pushed harder, I and Ness's power growing more assertive and brighter, overpowering the evil. I could feel the victory within my grasp.

Then, suddenly, searing pain tore through my mind. A whisper, soft and insidious, wormed its way into my thoughts. It was Damian speaking directly into my mind. "Flynn… remember who you are. What you did."

Images flashed before my eyes— images of Millie, her face twisted in pain, the moment of her death, his hands covered in her blood, his dagger plunged deep into her chest. I felt as my grip began to falter, my strength wavering.

"No…" I muttered, trying to bring myself out of the trance Damian was trying to suck me in. "No, that wasn't me… that was… your trick…"

But the images grew stronger, images of Millie's corpse laying there, blood pooling out as demons feasted on her corpse, peeling her skin off, leaving nothing but bones. "You killed her, Flynn," Damian whispered. "You were too weak, too blind, and you will kill again. This time being the brother you took into this battle selfishly."

Ness's voice cut through the fog. "Flynn! Stay with me!"

But I couldn't hear him. I was trapped in the nightmare, the guilt, the shame. The dagger slipped from my fingers, clattering onto the ground.

Damian's laughter filled my mind. "Yes, that's right, Flynn. Give into the darkness; it is where you belong."

And then, with a swift, calculated move, I was broken from the trance by Damian. Damian's hand shot forward, black energy wrapping around my throat, lifting me off the ground as I kicked and squirmed, my hands clawing at the energy that was constricting my air pipe. Ness lunged forward but was struck back by a blast of dark magic made by Damian, sending him flying into the mountain behind them.

"Stay out of this, boy!" Damian snarled. "This is between me and Flynn."

My vision began to blur, black spots dancing at the edges. I felt as the life began to drain from my body, the light dimming, and for a moment, I wondered if I would be able to see Millie again after my vision wholly faded.

But then, from somewhere deep within me, a voice spoke— a quiet, steady voice. "Remember who you are, Flynn. Remember why you fight."

My eyes snapped back open, divine light flaring within me. With a roar, I reached deep into myself, pulling on every ounce of divine power I possessed, and with a burst of holy light, shattered the darkness around my neck.

I landed on my feet, gasping for air, but my eyes locked on Damian. "You will not control me," I growled. "Not now, not ever."

Ness, seeing this, ran back towards me, drawing his sword and glaring at Damian.

Damian's eyes widened just for a fraction of a second, and I seized the moment. I grabbed my dagger from the ground and charged, the blade illuminated with power. I aimed straight for Damian's heart, but he was too quick, summoning a barrier of dark energy just in time.

Ness, although, went from the side, slashing Damian's arm. He let out a yelp, the barrier between them faltering.

Damian gritted his teeth, sweat beading on his brow. "A child will *not* defeat me!" He roared, holding his arms as the blood stained his sleeve.

Ness, who went back to stand beside me, raised his sword, his voice calm and steady. "Then maybe it's time you faced a man."

He unleashed a blast of divine light, and I followed suit, our powers combining in a brilliant explosion of light. The light collided with Damia, throwing him hard back against the ground.

Ness and I stood side by side, panting but resolute. The evil man struggled to his feet, having a mix of fury and disbelief. "This… this isn't over," He spat.

I took a step forward. "No, it's not. But you two have lost. You've lost the battle, and we will destroy your machine. The saints are already fighting past your wall of demons and ready to get to it." I said, my eyes narrowing.

Damian's face scrunched up. "I may have lost you, but there are others, **always others**."

Before I could react, Damian raised his hand, the ground beneath them shaking. A massive hand of darkness erupted from the Earth, grabbing Ness by the ankle and yanking him down. Ness cried out in shock, his sword slipping from his hand.

"*NO!*" I shouted, lunging forward to grab my brother, but it was too late. The darkness had swallowed him whole. I reached out, but the darkness receded, leaving only a hole where my brother had been.

I dropped to my knees, my heart racing while tears flooded my eyes as I grabbed onto my hair so tight that it began to rip out. "No… no, no, no… not again!" I screamed.

Damian stood over me, a triumphant smile on his face. "Awe, how sad. Another failure, another loss for you, Flynn."

I clenched my hands in my hair into fists, ripping my hair out even more as my breaths came out in ragged gasps. But across the battlefield, a new voice echoed— a voice filled with power and authority, a familiar voice.

"Enough, Damian!"

Lucifer descended from the sky, his dark wings outstretched, his eyes blazing with fury. He landed with a harsh impact, his presence commanding the attention of every demon and saint alike.

Lucifer's gaze swept over the scene, landing on me and Damian. "It seems you've had your fun with the boy, but now, it's time for me to take over." He said, glaring at Damian with a cold stare. "You've failed. You've lost your chance to defeat Flynn, and now, it's *my turn.*"

With a wave of his hand, Lucifer unleashed a torrent of dark energy that surged towards me. I raised my dagger, trying to summon my divine strength, but felt myself being pushed back, my power waning.

Lucifer's laughter filled the air, a deep sound that echoed with sinister intent. "You think you can even *fight* me? You can't even understand the power I withhold."

I struggled to rise, but my body was heavily drained of energy. I gleaned around, searching for my brother, but only found saints fierce in combat still with Lucifer's forces, the darkness seeming to close in around me.

Damian watched with a twisted smile as Lucifer's attack weakened me. "I told you, Flynn. You can't win.

My thoughts were a whirlwind of despair. My brother was gone, lost to darkness. Millie's face haunted me, and so did the fact that Michael was still being held in captivity. The weight of my losses was crushing me.

But then, a flicker of light— a spark of hope— caught my eye. One of the saints, a figure bathed in radiant light, approached me, cutting through the chaos with determined strides. It was a familiar face, one that I recognized.

The saint reached my side, extending a hand. Mr. Evans cared for Ness and me until we could care for ourselves, my found family. "We need you, Flynn. We need your strength."

Lucifer and Damian laughed as Mr. Evans tried to encourage me, but I couldn't help but feel warmth. I saw the unwavering determination in Mr. Evans's eyes, his light seemingly pushing back the darkness, renewing my strength.

"I'm here," I said, my voice firm and steady. "I will fight. For my brother, for Millie, for Michael, and all we've lost."

I rose to my feet, gripping my dagger with renewed courage. The darkness still surrounded me, but I could see the glimmer of hope. I turned to face Lucifer, my eyes flooded with bravery.

Lucifer's eyes narrowed his expression one of amusement. "You think you can still defeat me, Flynn? You're out of time."

I shook my head, my gaze unwavering. "It's not over, not yet."

With a yell, I ran forward, my dagger glowing again with divine light. The battle was far from over, but I would see it to the end.

The war raged on, and I fought valiantly alongside the saints, but the tide stayed against us. The machine still hadn't been broken, so Lucifer and Damian still had incredible strength.

I was bruised, Ness's sword lying alongside me, a faint glimmer of hope that kept me going. As I surveyed the battlefield, my eyes landed on the area of the Core the machine laid in, a reminder of why I was here to begin with.

"Flynn!" A voice shouted above the chaos. It was a tall and slender saint, blood-drenched their clothes, both theirs and the blood of demons. "We need to destroy the machine, now!"

I nodded, and I began to run. I ran as fast as I could to the building. Seeing this, Lucifer signaled for Damian to follow as he took care of the remaining surprisingly standing army of saints.

As I neared the machine, the ground of the building suddenly began to tremble, and an explosion of dark energy exploded right as I made my way up the stairs and into the room with the machine. The machine was on a balcony, a river of black water below it. I was thrown back against the railing at the explosion, my vision blurring momentarily.

Damian emerged from the depths of the explosion, his dark energy swirling around him like a storm. "You're too late again, Flynn!" Damian's voice boomed, filled with triumph.

I struggled to rise, my gaze falling on the machine, it's core pulsating with dark energy, sigils representing Lucifer scattered across it, carved into its metal. I grabbed my dagger and approached the machine, my eyes never leaving Damians.

In a swift movement, I gathered all my strength and slammed my dagger into the ground, the room filling with the blinding light just like two years ago, yet I didn't run this time. With all my strength, I plunged my dagger into the machine, and for some reason, I felt as if I was cutting into a cake instead of metal, effortlessly gliding down the metal and stabbing it repeatedly.

Suddenly, the man who happened to share the same blood as me appeared beside me. I winced in pain as Damian landed a blow to my stomach. I bent over, and once I did, he delivered a punch to my face. I struggled, got back up, and grabbed the cross I had buried deep inside my pocket.

"FATHER," I began, "PUT A BUBBLE OF PROTECTION TO WARD OFF THESE EVIL SPIRITS AROUND ME, AMEN."

As I said this, a bright light circled me.

"AAH-" Yelled Damian

With my limited time, I kicked a blow to his knees. As he fell to his knees, I pushed him.

I could see the fear in his eyes as he stumbled back to the ledge. As he attempted to regain his balance, he recited a spell of black magic. As soon as he finished, he fell off the edge of the Core. I winced in pain at the spell but soon felt a warm aura around me; it was finally the end.

I looked to the side where the machine was and watched as the dark power it gave began to dissipate, a new, blinding light that covered the area. The machine exploded, pushing me into a wall my head banging against it. My vision was blurred, but I could see the outline of someone.

"Took you long enough, dick." I immediately knew who it was.

I smiled and closed my eyes. "Michael, you know you can just say thank you," I said as tears flowed down my face from all the emotions that began to swallow me, happiness and sadness alike.

"Well, I shouldn't need to thank you when I brought you this," Micheal said, annoyed, but I could tell he was happy.

I opened my eyes and was immediately greeted by a hug from Ness. My eyes widened in surprise before I began to sob. I held onto Ness as tight as I could, scared that he'd disappear from me again at any moment. My brother also started to cry; we just held onto each other.

Then, we saw it. We saw the sun's light for the first time in seven years. Ness, Michael, and I rushed to the railing, watching as the clouded smokey sky cleared. Everyone below on the battlefield also stopped fighting, and Lucifer looked furious. We locked eyes, and he extended his dark wings.

"You... You little shit!" Lucifer said as he pushed off the ground, flying up to the three of us. I gripped my dagger, ready for him. "I will tear you apart piece by piece alive and—"

A bright light appeared before he could reach us and grabbed his ankle. Lucifer yelped as the light began to drag him down, the ground opening to reveal a fiery pit full of lava below the ground, where the fallen angel was going. Lucifer's screams echoed, and so did his demons, which began to burn to a cinder at the light of the sun. We all watched as Lucifer tried to escape but to no avail.

Then, a bright light appeared. The bright light appeared in all of my dreams, but it didn't talk; instead, it turned the world back. The dry, cracked lands and mountains began to grow grass flowers, and the river below us turned back from black to clear water, fish swimming in it. Trees began to grow around us, bees buzzed, lizards crawled, and I felt at home for the first time in seven years.

Chapter Fourteen

The once-battered world had begun to heal. The scars of the recent conflict were still visible, but the saints' relentless efforts and God's divine intervention had ushered in a new era of peace and rebuilding. The machine that had once served as a conduit for darkness was nothing more than ruins, and the weight of Lucifer's reign had been lifted.

In a small tranquil village lush valley, the remnants of the past conflict seemed like a distant memory. The village was a place of calm, with charming huts lined with blooming flowers and a gentle hum of everyday life. It was here, amidst the serenity of the new beginning, that Ness and I had found new solace and a semblance of normalcy.

The two of us had settled into a little hut at the edge of the village, surrounded by rolling fields and the gentle rustle of leaves. Our home was simple but warm, with a garden that we tended carefully. It was our sanctuary, our home that truly felt like home.

I stood in the garden. My hands were covered in soil as I worked on a vegetable patch. I wiped my face as I admired the growing produce. It was a stark contrast to the battle I fought fought, and I relished the simplicity of my new life.

Ness was nearby, constructing a birdhouse with extreme attention to detail. He had taken to crafting, finding solace in the rhythmic motion of his hands and the satisfaction of creating something beautiful from nothing but God's raw materials. The two of us worked side by side, and our strong bond was evident in our easy laughter and conversation.

As we worked, a familiar figure appeared at the edge of the village. Michael, the archangel, walked down a flight of stairs that ascended into Heaven. Usually, the angels would fly down, but since his wings were torn from him, he now needed to walk everywhere. Despite that, his presence still brought a sense of calm and familiarity.

"Hey, brats," Michael said with a smirk. He looked much better now. He now wore his old heavenly clothing angelic armor. His blonde hair wasn't greasy anymore, but long and styled, his hair down to his shoulders.

I looked up, my face lighting up with a smile as I saw my old friend. "Michael! It's great to see you. What brings you here?"

Michael walked gracefully up to them, his confidence evident. "I wanted to check in on y'all. It's been a minute since we last talked, and I've heard from the boss man things have been going well."

Ness looked up from his work, a smile spreading across his face. "It's been great, actually. It's strange how peaceful life is now."

Michael nodded, his gaze drifting over the peaceful surroundings. "It's well-deserved. The world is finally healing."

I wiped my hands on my pants, a thoughtful expression on my face. "It's hard to believe that in such a short time, so much has changed. Sometimes, it feels like a dream."

Michael chuckled softly. "Yeah, I getcha, but trust that it's real, all thanks to you two."

The conversation soon turned to a lighter topic as Michael joined Ness and me in our garden. We discussed the latest news from the village, the progress of the rebuilding efforts, and the small joys of everyday life. Michaels's visits began a cherished tradition, a reminder of the divine presence that had guided us through our darkest hours.

As the sun began to set, Ness and I prepared a simple meal of fresh vegetables and bread. We gathered around a wooden table outside, enjoying the sunlight they had once taken for granted.

Michael took a seat with us, his presence adding a sense of warmth and familiarity to the evening. Our table was filled with laughter and conversation as we shared past stories and reminisced about our past adventures.

After the meal, as the stars began to shine, Ness and I took a moment to reflect on our journey. We stood together on a nearby hill overlooking our small village, where roughly only five other families lived alongside us.

I turned to my brother, my expression one of contentment. "I never thought we'd find peace like this. It's more than I ever hoped for."

Ness nodded, his gaze fixed on the stars above. "We fought hard for it, but now, it's time to cherish this new life and beginning we've been given."

Michael joined the two of us, his presence a reminder of the journey we had gone through. "You've both earned this. The world is saved because of your sacrifices; *I'm* saved because of your sacrifices."

As we stood together, the quiet of the evening embracing us, I felt a deep sense of gratitude. The battles were over, the darkness had been vanquished, and now, in this tranquil moment, I could finally sink into the peace I had fought so hard to obtain.

The stars above seemed to shimmer with a sense of promise, a reminder that even im the darkest of times, there was always hope.

Acknowledgments

Writing this book has been a journey of discovery and growth, and I owe a great deal of gratitude to the many people who have supported me along the way.

First and foremost, I want to thank my family—my dad, my mom, and my little sister Layla—for their unwavering patience, love, and encouragement. Your belief in me has been a constant source of strength, and I can't thank you enough.

To my old English teachers, Mr. Cordes and Mrs. Telles, your insightful feedback and a keen eye for detail transformed this manuscript into something much better than I could have imagined. Thank you for your dedication and expertise.

Finally, to my girlfriend Norah, who provided support and inspiration along the way, your kindness and enthusiasm have constantly reminded me why I embarked on this journey.

To everyone who has contributed to this process, I am profoundly grateful.

A Sneak Peak For:
Eclipse of Realms

Chapter One

The Citadel floated at the center of all things, a nexus where reality folded upon itself, an anchor to the countless realms that shined like stars across the cosmos. The Citadel was woven from the essence of the multiverse itself— walls of light and shadow, reflecting the intense struggle it was meant to preserve. Within its vast, crystal halls, the Guardians went about their day.

Elaria, the Guardian of Positivity, was awake before the sun awoke. However, in the Citadel, the morning was more of a feeling than a time of day despite the light that the multiverse inhabitants called the sun. She stepped into the Hall of Radiance, a chamber that pulsed with a soft, golden glow. Her presence alone brightened the room even more, her mere existence a beacon of warmth and hope. She was a tall, slender figure with long, silver hair that flowed behind her, and her bright gold eyes, the color of the sunrise, gleamed with kindness that seemed to radiate from her soul.

She moved to the hall's center, where a significant, hovering globe displayed the endless universes under their care. She raised her hand, and the globe shimmered in response, expanding outwards, revealing countless worlds and their fates. Her hand hovered over a small, dim world at the edge of the map— a world that she had visited many times before, a world that only knew sorrow and grief. There were many worlds in the multiverse, some that could only feel happiness, some that had endless rage, and the inhabitants always fighting. There were even some places where humans spoke through music and others where animals ruled the world, with no humans in sight.

"Poor souls," Elaria murmured, closing her eyes. She reached out, her mind brushing against the globe, feeling the universe's pain. With a deep breath, she channeled her energy, her palms beginning to glow as a golden liquid poured from her fingertips, flowing into the world below.

For a moment, she could see through the eyes of a child in a dimly lit room, alone and weeping. She sent the child a wave of comfort and warmth, her hair floating and glowing. Slowly, the child's tears ceased, and a small smile formed on her lips, a spark of warmth igniting her heart.

She continued to weave her light into the universe, feeling the ripple of calm spread through its inhabitants. In that moment, sorrow lifted within the world, even if only for a little.

"Another day, another burden lightened," she whispered with a gentle smile, lowering her hand.

As Elaria left the Hall of Radiance, she sensed a familiar presence approaching—her twin brother, Elgaron, the Guardian of Negativity. Elaria's aura was warm and golden, and Elagron's was a deep indigo, the color of a midnight sky just before a storm. His dark hair fell around his face and shoulders in rough waves; his violet eyes seemed to pierce the air as if constantly searching for flaws, a crack in the world.

"Elgaron," Elaria greeted, her voice light, though she could feel the air become heavy around him.

"Sister," Elgaron replied, his tone more measured. "You've been busy. I can already feel the positivity flowing through the realms."

Elaria smiled. "I do what I can to keep the balance. Though I'm sure, you've already noticed the many places where your influence lingers."

Elgaron chuckled, a low sound like distant thunder. "Balance, yes. It seems we've both had quite the productive evening."

The tension between the two siblings was ever-present, a familiar tug-of-war neither could avoid. Despite their differences, Elaria loved her brother deeply, even if his methods often disturbed her. She looked over his shoulder to see Verathia and Kalaron approaching, their footsteps silent on the glass floor.

Verathia, the Guardian of Creation, appeared as a figure of infinite elegance. Her eyes were sharp, and her expression thoughtful. She always considered the endless possibilities of what could be. She lowered her head in greeting.

"Elaria, Elgaron," Verathia began, her voice fluid as a flowing stream. "There is something… different in the realms today. I've sensed disruptions in the universes—flickers like a dying light."

Elaria frowned, her bright demeanor dimming slightly. "I've felt something as well. It's faint, but it's there."

Elagron crossed his arms, his gaze hardening. "Disruptions are to be expected. Nothing stays stable forever. Perhaps it's time to let those universes come to their natural end."

Verathia shook her head. "It's not just the dying worlds; new worlds are feeling this as well, ones that should be full of life and potential… but something is holding them back as if they are waiting for something."

Kalaron, Guardian of Destruction, stood silently, his golden eyes overseeing the others as he stood beside Verathia. He was a figure of quiet strength, his charcoal skin littered with scars and tattoos, each from a realm he had laid to rest. "If there is a disruption, we must find its source," he said simply. "We must maintain the balance."

Elaria nodded. "Then we will do what we always do. We will watch, and we will act as needed."

But in the back of her mind, a shadow of unease lingered. She couldn't shake the feeling that something was coming, something beyond their understanding.

As the Guardians returned to their respective quarters, the Citadel seemed to hum with unseen energy. Elaria returned to her chambers, but her thoughts were relentless. She stared out the window of her room and down onto the multiverse below, her hands resting against the cool surface of the glass.

Far below, the universes continued their dance, some flourishing with light and life, others dimming as they approached their inevitable end. Elaria felt a faint flicker of fear for the first time in centuries. Something was changing, something she couldn't yet name.

In the distance reaches of the Citadel, a shadow moved— a whisper of force unseen, waiting patiently for the right time to strike.

The Guardians, unaware, continued with their eternal duties, oblivious to the hidden hand that would soon test the strength of their unity and the true meaning of balance in a universe where even the brightest light casts a shadow.

Elaria left her room and wandered the winding corridors of the Citadel, her thoughts heavy with Verathias words. Disruptions, she had said, subtle flickers in the fabric of new and old worlds alike. The notion gnawed at her; it was rare for Verathia to express such concern. She considered seeking her out again, but Elaria knew pressing the matter too soon might stir unnecessary worry.

Instead, she decided to check on one of the more volatile universes that always seemed to linger on the brink of death.

Her touch may be needed there. She made her way down the Hall of Radiance, reaching the globe that shone a soft gold. She reached out to touch the globe but felt a pull—an unexpected rush of cold; a shiver went down her spine. A dark and heavy shadow arose in her peripheral vision. She recognized it at once.

"Elgaron," she murmured, her voice clear against the stillness. With a sigh, she followed the shadow's trail, making her way down to the Hall of Shades, a dimly lit chamber where her brother resided, often withdrawing his powers here.

As she stepped through the archway, the warmth of her presence clashed against the cold, comber atmosphere of the hall. The walls were made of a dark, polished, cracked stone, and the light seemed to shy away from them, leaving the room in darkness.

Elgaron stood at the center, his form partially obscured by an aura of indigo and deep violet. He did not turn as she entered, but she knew he could sense her. He stared at a small, shifting mass of dark energy floating above his outstretched hands—an orb that seemed to pulse with negative emotions: grief, anger, and despair.

"Playing with shadows again, brother?" Elaria called out, her tone light, though a hunt of tension crept in.

Elgaron's shoulders tensed, but he did not turn to face her. "They're not just shadows," he replied, his voice low and resonant. They are the essence of what you deny—the part of life you desperately try to erase."

Elaria approached slowly, her golden light fighting the shadows on the walls. "I don't deny them, Elgaron," she said softly. "I acknowledge them. But I believe in helping others find a way through despair, not let them drown in it."

Finally, he turned, his eyes gleaming like distant stars in the dimness of the hall. "And yet, you weaken the balance every time you do so. The more you brighten one side, the darker the other becomes. Do you not see that?"

She took a deep breath, keeping her voice calm. "I see it. I've always seen it. But what you call balance, I call despair. You let people suffer in their darkest moments, feeding on their misery when they could be—"
"Could be what?" he cut her off, his voice sharp. "Living in a delusion? Floating on a raft of false hope? Elaria, you make them believe there is light when there is none. You give them… illusions."

She flinched at his words, and her golden aura flickered and dimmed momentarily. She steadied herself. "And you, Elgaron, make them believe there is no light. You are the reason they see only darkness."

Elgaron stepped closer, his eyes narrowing. "They need to see the darkness, to know it, to accept it. Only then can they truly understand themselves. Without me, they'd live in ignorance of what really is."

Elaria's heart tightened. This was always their argument— a battle of philosophies, light versus shadow, with neither willing to allow an open mind to listen genuinely to what the other says. She could feel the familiar frustration but fought to keep in check. "And yet, Elgaron, how many of them have you left broken? How many worlds have fallen because they could not bear the weight of your truth?"

He turned away from her, his hands clenching into fists. "I do not break them. I reveal them. I reveal their flaws, their fears... their truths. If they shatter, it is because they are already cracked."

She stepped forward, her hand hovering just above his shoulder, a touch she hesitated to give. "Maybe... maybe they need more than just the truth," she spoke softly. "Maybe all they need is hope."

Elgaron stiffened, his jaw tightening. "Hope," he scoffed. "Hope is a fragile thing, Elaria. It shatters the moment reality touches it."

"And yet, it's our strongest force," she insisted. "It's what keeps them moving forward, even in the darkest night."

Elgaron's shoulders tensed, but his expression remained guarded. "Your light blinds you, sister. There are things in this multiverse even your hope can not reach."

A long silence settled between them, filled with the distant hum of the Citadel's energy flowing around them; Elaria felt the weight of her brother's words, the depth of their disagreement. They had been like this for as long as she could remember— complete opposites, always pulling in different directions. She wondered, not for the first time if they would ever truly see eye to eye.

She took a step back, her eyes locked on her brother. "I'm not here to argue with you, Elgaron. I'm here to help. Whatever happens in the multiverse, we must face it together."

Elgaron sighed, his shoulders relaxing just for a fraction of a second. "Together, yes," he murmured, though his tone was uncertain. "But don't be naive, Elaria. We are not the same, and we never will."

Elaria gave him a soft, sad smile. "Maybe that's why we need each other."

He didn't reply, but his silence was softer than before. The tension between them seemed to ease briefly, if only slightly. Elaria turned to leave, casting one last glace over her shoulder.

"Just... think about it, Elgaron," she said quietly. "We're stronger together, you know that."

Without waiting for his response, she left the hall, her mind spinning with thoughts. She knew their bond was frayed, strained by the centuries of conflict, but deep down, she still loved him. For whatever lay ahead, she knew they'd need each other.

As she walked away, Elgaron remained in the shadows, his gaze fixed on the orb hovering above his palm. For a brief moment, his expression softened, a flicker of doubt passing through his violet eyes. Then, with a wave of his hand, the orb vanished, swallowed by the darkness surrounding him.

Elaria made her way out of her brother's quarters and into the halls of Citadel. She knew she'd need to speak with Verathia and Kalaron soon— she wanted more insight about this anomaly, and the two other guardians would give her clear answers.

Turning a corner, she came upon Verathia's chamber, a vast space that seemed to breathe with life. The walls were a living mural, shifting and changing with different vibrant images every second. The chamber was alive with energy, a constant hum of creation vibrating through the air.

Verathia stood at the center, her form rippling with ever-changing colors, like sunlight passing through water. She walked in fluid motion; each step was a dance. As Elaria approached, she saw Verathia deep in thought, her hand tracing patterns over a model for a new universe based in outer space.

"Verathia," Elaria called softly, not wanting to disturb the Guardian of Creation's concentration. Verathia looked up, her face breaking into a warm, enigmatic smile.

"Elaria!" she greeted, her voice a melody that matched the room's energy. "You've come to check in with me?"

Elaria nodded, returning the smile. "I wanted to hear more about the disruptions you felt earlier. I sense them, too, but... they feel elusive, like shadows in the corner of my vision."

Verathia nodded, her expression turning thoughtful. "Yes, they are subtle, aren't they? Almost like ripples in a pond—small at first, but growing, spreading." She turned to her model, her fingers tracing the edges. "I've seen these ripples in universes that were... altered somehow, changed by forces unseen. But this feels different. More deliberate."

Elaria's brow furrowed. "Deliberate? Do you think something—someone— is causing it?"

Verathia's eyes flickered with a strange light, a gleam gone as quickly as it appeared. "I don't know," she replied, her tone measured. "But I intend to find out. We must keep a close eye on the realms and see if these disruptions grow stronger or if there is a change in nature."

There was something in her voice, a note that Elaria couldn't quite place. A determination that was sharp, interested in this ripple. "I'm sure we will uncover the truth soon. The multiverse has its way of revealing itself closely."

Elaria nodded, and before she could push the topic further, Kalaron appeared in the doorway, his towering form framed by the soft glow of the chamber's living walls.

Kalaron moved with a quiet, deliberate grace. His striking gold eyes seemed to see everything yet revealed nothing. His expression was calm and serene, a stark contrast to the role he played, considering his role as the Guardian of Destruction. He was the end of everything, yet he carried it with dignity.

"Elaria, Verathia," Kalaron greeted, his deep voice rumbling. "I sensed a discussion of importance. Has something changed?"

Verathia turned to him, her face unreadable. "We were just speaking of the disruptions in the realms. I feel they may be growing stronger, more deliberate."

Kalaron's gaze shifted between them, his expression thoughtful. "Disruptions are inevitable, but deliberate? That implies intent... and intent means something or someone is behind it."

Elaria nodded. "That's what we're worried about. If a force is at work, we need to be ready."

Kalaron crossed his arms, his posture calm but alert. "Then we must remain vigilant. If there is something at play here, it will reveal itself in time. Until then, we should continue our duties and maintain balance as best as possible."

Verathia smiled at him, an amusement flicker in her eyes. "Always the sensible one, Kalaron," she said lightly. "But you're right. We must wait and watch, and when the time comes, we will act."

Elaria watched them both, sensing the unspoken understanding between Verathia and Kalaron. Their roles were intertwined; creation and destruction were two opposites, much like positivity and negativity. But where Elaria and Elgaron clashed, Verathia and Kalaron seemed to move in harmony, each complementing the other's purpose.

Their conversation was interrupted by a sudden tremor in the Citadel, a deep, resonant vibration that seemed to pulse through the very core of its structure. Elaria felt it first, and there was a faint tingling in her fingertips to the rest of her body. She exchanged a quick, concerned glance with Kalaron, whose brow furrowed in confusion.

"What was that?" Kalaron asked, his golden eyes narrowing. Before anyone could answer, a low hum filled the room—a deep, rumbling sound that seemed to come from everywhere. The walls of Verathia's chamber flickered, the images of verdant forests and vibrant stars suddenly dimming, the colors draining as if a shadow had fallen over them.

Verathia's expression grew sharper, her usual calm demeanor replaced by an alert intensity. "The Multiverse is shifting," she whispered, her eyes widening. "Something is… wrong."

Elaria closed her eyes, reaching out with her senses to feel the balance of realms. She instantly felt a rupture, a tear in the fabric of existence. A universe was being... undone. Not by time or entropy, but by force—something, or someone, was tearing it apart.

Kalaron's eyes darkened, his voice grim. "A universe is dying," he said, his tone heavy with concern. "But not in natural ways... this is different. Violent. Deliberate."

Verathia's face tightened, her lips forming a thin line. "Show us," she commanded, and with a wave of her hand, a giant, floating orb of colors appeared in the center of the room. The orb swirled with color like paint, slowly clearing to reveal devastation.

They saw a universe in its death throes—a brilliant masterpiece of stars and planets tearing apart at the seams. Energy crackled wildly, and entire galaxies collapsed into themselves as if consumed by an unseen force. Elaria's heart sank at the sight; she had seen universes end before, but this... this was different. This was destruction without reason—a senseless, brutal end.

Kalaron's jaw clenched. "Who could do this?" He murmured, his voice a low growl.

Elaria's gaze remained fixed on the image, her mind racing. "Whoever—or whatever— is behind this, they are strong. To tear apart a universe like this... it takes great power."

Verathia's eyes were locked on the scene of destruction, her face calm but expression unreadable. "This is… unprecedented," she said slowly, her voice soft yet resonant. "A force of this magnitude… we would have felt it before now. How did they remain hidden?"

Her eyes flickered with a strange light, a glint that seemed to dance in the depths of her irises. She turned to the others, her face carefully composed. "We must go," she said, her voice decisive. "We must investigate this anomaly ourselves. If there is a force capable of this, it threatens the very fabric of existence."

Kalaron nodded, already preparing to leave. "Agreed," he said. "If this force is as powerful as it seems, we cannot let it roam unchecked."

Elaria felt a surge of urgency, her power humming in response to the chaotic energy of the dying universe. She could feel the echoes of fear, despair, and confusion coming from the distant realm, which fueled her determination. "Let's go," she said firmly, turning to Verathia. "You're right. We need to act now."

Verathia nodded, a small enigmatic smile playing at the corner of her lips. "Of course," she agreed, her voice smooth. "We can't waste a moment. The balance is at stake."

Kalaron went to fetch Elgaron, who came in swiftly and prepared to leave. The four guardians moved as one, their forms becoming blurs of shadows and light as they vanished from the chamber, leaving Citadel behind.

The orb continued to show the dying universe, its last remnants collapsing into a void of darkness. A faint glimmer of light lingered in the corner of the room where Verathia had been standing— a single spark, almost unnoticeable, pulsing faintly like a heartbeat before flickering out.

About The Author

Despite her years, Bayli Peck is a 15-year-old writer and aspiring criminologist passionate about storytelling. Growing up in a city in California, Bayli has always found solace and inspiration in books, which sparked her journey into writing.

Her first published novel, Eternal Nightfall, reflects her keen observations of teenage life and her vibrant imagination. Bayli enjoys sketching, playing the piano, and caring for her nephews and niece when she's not crafting compelling narratives.

Despite her young age, Bayli has been writing since she was five, always showing and reading her stories to family and friends. She dreams of continuing to write stories that resonate with readers of all ages and hopes to inspire other young people to follow their passions.

Bayli lives with her family and their two mischievous dogs. She is currently working on her next book while balancing high school, college, and various hobbies.

Made in the USA
Columbia, SC
17 September 2024